Sink Into Her

A Sunshine Key Romance

Elaine J Daniels

To anyone who needed a sapphic kraken in their life. This one is for you.

Content Warnings

While this story has a HEA, there are some content warnings to consider if you have any triggers.

This book contains explicit sex scenes featuring tentacles, kidnapping, mild violence, threats of violence against one of the FMCs, threats of violence by one of the FMCs, and threatened gun violence (not by the FMCs).

Chapter 1
Alex

"Hey, Siri, remind me not to watch horror movies before bed," I mutter into my iPhone as I unlock the gate to Sunshine's Seaside Resort pool. I don't know why the resort uses the term 'seaside' when the entire island is so tiny that you can always smell the low tide, but I don't ask questions I'm not paid to ask. Seaside Resort may pay on the higher end, but pool managers aren't exactly swimming in cash.

"I didn't get that," Siri responds. "Could you try again?"

I sigh. "Unhelpful as usual."

My big sister, Avery, is a major horror movie fan. She's constantly recommending the latest and greatest scary movies, and I love her so much that I watch them despite losing sleep for a few days afterward. Last night's movie was some modern take on *Jaws* with an even more gigantic shark.

One would think that growing up on an island in the Florida Keys would temper any fear of sharks and whatever other beasts lurk beneath the surface because I don't know anyone who has ever been attacked by anything larger than a crab. But alas, that's not the case when it comes to movies. I blame the creepy music.

I stroll into my office, toss my backpack on my desk, and then use a large claw clip in the shape of a shark to roughly pin up the rat's nest I call my hair. I should laugh, considering the circumstances, but I'm too tired and hot. It's going to be a scorcher today. I bet the water isn't even going to be pleasant to swim in.

The clock reads 8:30 a.m. This gives me an hour of quiet to complete my paperwork before the lifeguards arrive. My staff, consisting primarily of teenagers, are loud and distracting with their raging hormones, causing them to focus on flirting with each other more than paying attention to patrons. I can't even be mad at them; I once was a teen with raging hormones.

The younger ones all think I'm mean, while the older ones who have been here a few years now know that I'm fair. Maybe a little abrasive, but fair. Forgive me for wanting a little order in my life. But before I can hole up in my office with my second cup of black coffee, I need to do a water level check for the chlorine and PH balance.

I step onto the pool deck, and something dark at the bottom of the pool's deep end catches my eye. A cold sweat breaks out across my skin despite the summer heat. *What is that? Is it a person?* My thoughts race as I rush to the pool's edge. Maybe it's just a lounge chair some drunk resort guest tossed in. But the pit of my stomach knows that something isn't right.

The floating fan of hair under the water confirms my worst fear. I don't even waste time grabbing a lifeguard tube from the locked equipment room. It would take too long. I dive in and claw 12 feet down to the vaguely human-shaped shadow. Every second is precious if they are still alive.

When I reach the figure, even through the blur of the water, the limbs don't look like human legs. What the fuck am I about to pull above the surface? Maybe it's the water playing tricks on me, but there's no time to worry about that. I slide my elbows under the body's armpits and attempt to kick off the bottom of the pool, however, the body's weight prevents my ascent. They're like a sack of bricks in my arms. I try again, but all I manage to do is flail pathetically.

We're both fucked if I don't summon the strength to get this person off the bottom of the pool. If I don't concentrate, we'll both die. I reposition myself to get better leverage. With a powerful push of both legs, I eventually manage to propel us off the bottom of the pool.

My thighs and lungs scream with effort as I fight my way to the surface. But I can't give up. If I'm going to drown, at least I can say I gave it my all.

Relief floods over me when I reach the water's surface as I suck in gulps of sweet air. But it's not time to celebrate just yet. I still have a life in my arms. I keep the head of the body above the surface as I desperately kick to the pool's edge. My years of not only lifeguarding but training other lifeguards take over. I position the body safely with its head and arms above the pool gutter before hopping out. High on adrenaline, I drag them from the water with a pained grunt. I collapse on my hands and knees next to the body.

My jaw drops when I finally get a good look at the body. The extra limbs that didn't look like human legs under the water are actually six weakly writhing tentacles with suckers! What the fuck did I just rescue? And the tentacles aren't the only strange thing about them. They have ocean-blue skin that fades into shades of seafoam, speckled with deep blue spots, and ears that look like fish fins.

Shit! I can't freak out yet! I still need to scan the body for signs of life and injury. They might be some kind of tentacle monster, but even monsters deserve to live, right? They must be alive since their tentacles are wriggling. But wait, don't octopus tentacles still move even after they've been detached from the body?

I have no idea how long they were in the water or if that even matters. It only takes a few minutes to drown, but can octopus people even drown? Should I try CPR? Where is their heart even located?

What if they actually need water? They were unconscious when I found them and they're still not showing any sign of life, so I'm assuming they need help. No time to overthink it. I'll just treat them like a human since they have a humanish face and upper-body structure.

As I watch for their chest to rise and fall, I bring my ear to their mouth to feel for breath. But I have no time to judge when a wet rasp from their lips startles me. I struggle to keep my balance. A webbed hand grips my wrist, keeping me from falling over.

The most beautiful golden eyes I've ever seen peer up at me. The color shimmers like gold dust in liquid around thick horizontal pupils.

"You're alive!" The outburst is strangled in my throat.

The grip on my wrist tightens. "Don't let them take my heart." Their voice is low and barely audible.

My mind races as it attempts to understand what they just said. "Who? And what are they taking?"

Just as suddenly as their hand grasped me, they let go. Their eyes lose focus before closing.

"No!" I gently tap their cheek. "Don't fall asleep."

Another quick vital check confirms they are still breathing. I scurry to my feet and sprint to my office to find my phone. With shaking hands, I unlock the screen and type in 9-1-1, but I freeze before I hit the call button.

How am I going to explain an octopus person on my pool deck? They look like some kind of octopus centaur. Octo-taur? Cen-topus? Wait. Cen-topus makes it sound like they have 100 tentacles. That's not right.

Whatever. I can't call first responders. For some reason, I have a soft spot for this creature I risked my life to rescue. I don't want to see them hurt and in the hands of the government, where they will most likely put them in a lab and stick things up their butt. Do octopi have butts?

And what if the government hands them off to the wrong people? They mentioned something about their heart being taken. That would be worse than anal probing, right? I have to protect this creature at all costs. Both their heart and their butt.

"Stop thinking about butts, Alex," I mutter to myself.

I pocket my phone and rush back onto the pool deck, hoping they're still alive. The creature lies motionless on the deck. A nervous lump forms in my throat as I crouch next to them to check their vital signs, and I breathe a sigh of relief. They are stable – unconscious – but stable.

My relief is temporary. I can't leave them on the pool deck for my staff to see. That would be a disaster.

The clock reads 8:47 a.m. I have little time to figure out what to do with this creature before my staff arrives. I dart to the equipment room to grab a backboard. If I can strap them in, I will have an easier time dragging them to my office, where I can hide them until I figure out what the *fuck* I am going to do.

When I attempt to move them onto the backboard, they

don't budge. Not even an inch. I wouldn't call myself weak. I hit the gym every day after work, and I don't skip leg day. This shouldn't be so hard. I attempt it again, but am unsuccessful. This octopus person is heavy. I can only assume the six wriggling tentacles add a lot of extra weight.

Adjusting my position, I try again. No luck. All I have to show for my efforts is a layer of sweat on my brow.

My shoulders sag in defeat. I could barely get them out of the pool. How the fuck am I going to do this alone? I forgot, like an idiot, how difficult it would be to move someone so heavy by myself.

I take the time to inhale and exhale a few calming breaths. I can do this. I saved this mysterious creature once. I can do it again. The hardest part is out of the way. I square my shoulders.

Let's fucking go!

By the time I have them on the backboard and strapped in, I'm huffing, puffing, and drenched in sweat. My panic was forgotten in the wake of physical exertion. I leave their bottom half unsecured, hoping I ratcheted them tight enough everywhere else, because there is no way the straps are going around their thick tentacles. The last thing I need is them sliding off as I drag them to my office. That would suck, and I don't mean the tentacle suction kind of suck.

Thankfully, they stay on the backboard. Their tentacles scrape along the rough concrete of the pool deck. Here's to hoping they are a kind monster who will forgive me for the abrasions and not use it as an excuse to eat me. I don't want to be monster chow.

Why did this creature have to end up in the bottom of my pool? Couldn't they have found another one? Or better yet, stayed in the ocean. But it's too late now. I'm committed to saving them.

When we make it to my office, I slam the door behind me and collapse in my desk chair, chest heaving, taking a few moments to drink water and collect myself. I have been trying to take this morning one step at a time, but now it's finally settling in that I have bitten off more than I can chew.

How long can I keep them in my office before I get the chance to sneak them back to the ocean? Should I even be putting them back in the ocean? I'm at a total loss. And what am I going to do when they regain consciousness? I could barely handle them unconscious. *Shit. I'm so fucked.*

To better understand what I'm up against, I examine the creature. Their skin color, six tentacles, and webbed fingers are otherworldly, but they also have very human attributes. They are pretty with high cheekbones, full lips, and a delicate rounded chin. I lean forward and admire their long lashes, and up close, I can see their dark, long hair is actually green, like seaweed.

My gaze wanders to their physique. They have the lean musculature of an Olympic swimmer with a slight swell in their chest that reminds me of human breasts.

Did I rescue a female octopus person?

I know for a fact that octopi don't have breasts, but I know I need to stop thinking of them as an octopus. They have some human features and should be treated as such, which means unstrapping them. I don't want them to wake up scared, confused, and restrained.

I scurry to grab a spare lifeguard tube and towels from the lost and found to build a makeshift cot and pillow before carefully sliding them onto the bed. It's not the most comfortable, but it's better than the hard plastic of the backboard or the concrete floor.

There's just enough time for one last vitals check. Their

steady breathing and pulse make me feel confident enough to leave them alone. My staff should be arriving any minute, and I don't want anyone to come looking for me. They would freak if they found this monster in my office.

Just before I step out of the door, I arrange all the random snacks I keep in my backpack next to them in case they wake up hungry. I hope they like bananas and granola bars. Can octopi even eat stuff like that? Damnit. Not octopi. But also not human.

Ugh. This is making my head hurt.

When I open the door to my office, Staci, one of my older lifeguards, greets me. She's home for the summer before starting her senior year of college. Her no-nonsense attitude makes her one of my favorites, but I can't tell her that or the staff will think I've gone soft. It also helps that she's the only staff member I don't have to peer up at to look in the eye. Being only five feet tall has its drawbacks when everyone towers over you.

She twirls a strand of long ink-black hair in her fingers and blows a large bubble of her chewing gum. "What's up with the water levels not being checked?"

I scoff. "You know I do that as a favor. The openers technically have to check the PH balance and chlorine."

She snaps her gum. "Fine. I'll do it." Staci looks me up and down. "Why are you wet? You didn't go swimming alone, did you? What about your number one rule? Never go swim—"

"Never go swimming alone. I know. I—uh—fell in the pool." The lie feels like cotton in my mouth. I don't make a habit of lying. It makes a mess of things, and I also suck at it.

Her eyes narrow. My heart rate spikes. Does she know I'm not telling the truth?

She snorts. "Tragic. Go change into dry clothes. I'll handle the other lifeguards."

I offer her a rare smile. "Thank you, Staci."

Staci jabs a finger in my direction. "You owe me."

"Of course." I hold back a chuckle. "I wouldn't expect this kindness from you for free."

Once Staci turns the corner, I reenter my office to grab my spare uniform. I don't want to draw more attention to my wet clothing. Typically, I would change in here, but I would be mortified if the octopus person caught me with my pants down. I sneak into the staff bathroom, peel off my wet clothes, and slip on the white polo and khaki shorts over a dry swimsuit.

The work day goes by without a hitch despite the insane morning I just had. Somehow, I keep it together as I handle my typical duties. I get a few complaints from patrons about how warm the water is, but I can do nothing about that as I don't control the freaking weather. The chlorine burns off in the heat, so I have to keep a close eye on the water levels. It all feels so mundane now that I know there are real-life monsters in the world.

Between assisting in answering patron questions, relieving the lifeguards when needed, and sending hourly reports to the resort manager, I sneak into my office to check on the octopus person. Their vitals remain stable, but they still haven't stirred. As the day drags on, I get more anxious about it. I jump every time someone says my name. Every playful scream from a child sounds like one of terror, and I'm constantly sweating, even in the air conditioning of the snack shack.

I'm zoning out thinking about my predicament when there is a tap on my shoulder, startling me. Carter, my assistant manager, is here for the evening shift.

"Alex, babe! You alright?" He already has his shirt off, subtly flexing his eight-pack abs.

I roll my eyes. "We've been over this. Don't call me 'babe.' And I'm fine, just in a weird mood."

"Yeah. Staci said you fell in the pool this morning."

"I did. It kind of put me in a weird mindset." I cringe to myself at my half-truth.

"Well, I'm here now. You can take off."

I can't leave yet. There's still an unconscious body in my office. "I might be a little longer. I have a lot of paperwork to catch up on." The lie stumbles from my mouth. I relax my posture, hoping to look casual and not like someone who just told a big fat fib.

"I can handle it," he offers.

"It's okay." I smile. "Thank you, Carter."

I clap him on the shoulder to show him my gratitude and rush to my office before he catches on to my obvious fabrication. When I open the door, my eyes snap straight to the makeshift bed, and my heart races. It's empty.

Did they escape? Is there an octopus person hiding somewhere in my office, waiting for the perfect opportunity to overpower and eat me? I fish the utility knife I always keep on me out of my pocket, brandishing it like a weapon, ready to fight back.

"I assume you are the resident of this humble abode?"

The melodic yet husky voice startles me out of my panic. The most beautiful woman I've ever seen sits at my desk, completely naked, her pale skin peeking through a curtain of long dark-green hair. She looks familiar, but I can't put my finger on how until I look into her eyes. I'll never forget those golden eyes, even if the pupils are no longer horizontal and not currently shimmering as if infused with magic.

It's the octopus person but in a human body.

My jaw drops. "Who... What...are you?"

She smiles as if holding back a giggle. "I'm a kraken. That's the only thing I know for sure. The rest is kind of fuzzy," she says with a slight accent I can't quite place. Maybe Nordic.

A kraken? Like the giant squid monster from the movies? Yesterday, I would have laughed in her face. But I pulled a six-tentacled creature out of the pool this morning. I have a million questions racing through my head. Important ones include asking her for clarification on the whole 'kraken' thing and how she's now a human.

"What's your name?" I croak, unable to articulate anything with more substance.

The smile drops from her lips. "I don't know. I was hoping you could tell me."

Chapter 2
Kraken

T*hirty Minutes Prior...*

Ugh! The pain in my head is unbearable. Why does it ache so much?

Wait a second.

Something isn't right. And it isn't just my headache. There is no push and pull of the ocean's tide. I'm on dry land. But how did that happen?

"Oh no," I whisper, clutching my heaving chest. I can't remember anything! Where am I? Who am I? What is my name? Blank, after blank, after blank.

What am I going to do?

Taking in my surroundings, I try to ground myself. I'm in a room of some sort, with various pieces of framed papers on the dull gray walls. Am I a prisoner? There is only one way to find out, and that is to try the single metal door. Relief washes over me when the handle turns, allowing me to peek outside. Should I make a break for it? No. I need to remain cautious and calm. Who knows what kind of situation I'm in?

I suck in a breath when a human walks past the door,

muttering to themself in English about how it's too hot to be working. Memories come rushing back. While some humans are wonderful, others can be selfish, fearful creatures with a penchant for cruelty. Thankfully, the human isn't paying attention and breezes right past me. I say a silent prayer to the goddess for giving me such good instincts.

My tentacles relax from their tight coil as I close the door behind me with a soft click. The threat of the human is out of the way for now, but that doesn't solve my bigger problem. Is there another way to escape? My eyes dart around the room before landing on the pallet of rough fabric I was lying on when I woke.

Someone must have put me there. Did they want me to be comfortable? Maybe that same someone could help me figure out what happened to me?

But I need to look as unthreatening as possible if that someone is a human. Most humans don't know about krakens, and when confronted with one, they freak out. I can't have that.

An idea crackles through me like lightning on the ocean's surface. I can transform! All krakens possess basic glamor magic, so the process is simple enough. I just imagine myself as a human until my tentacles fuse, my sharp teeth become blunt, and my skin fades to the color of snow. It won't hold for long, but it will do for now.

I settle into the chair furthest from the door, and wait for my kind benefactor to return while I oscillate between trying to remember my name and telling myself everything will be okay. I chew my lip as I mutter, "Positive thoughts equal positive results."

There is no room for negativity in this current situation.

But the human who eventually walks through the door surprises me with her handsome face and soft body. It's like the clouds have parted to reveal the sun. My heart quickens. The way her face scrunches when she's confused is cute.

Were humans always this adorable? Or is it just her? I can't remember the last time I saw one, or any other living being, for that matter. There's something special about this human, I just know it.

But I quickly push those thoughts aside when she comes close to panicking. I have to get her emotions under control, or things can take a nasty turn. She can call other humans, and that would surely be the end of me.

"What do you mean you don't know your name?" she whispers, her fists clenched at her sides.

Uh oh. This can't be good. "Does that mean you don't know either?"

"Of course not!" she exclaims, mouth agape. "This is the first time I've seen you conscious since I pulled you out of the pool this morning!"

I take a deep breath. The human's fear makes my legs twitch, my tentacles eager to break free from this glamor. They don't like this form I'm forced to be in right now.

"What's your name?" I ask, softening my gaze and putting on my best soothing smile.

The human's eyes go wide before looking at the ground. "A-Alex."

What a cute name! I hold back the urge to squeal. Now really isn't the time to be gushing. "Well, Alex, I need you to tell me everything that happened this morning. But calmly. Can you do that for me?"

"Can you put on clothes first?" she asks, covering her eyes with her hands.

I look down at my nudity. Ah, that's right. Humans

prefer to cover themself with fabric. I giggle. "You humans are so prudish."

She finally looks me in the eyes with a glare. *Goddess. She's so cute!* Her skin is sun-kissed with freckles across her nose and cheeks. But her hazel eyes take my breath away even as they stare daggers into me.

"We're not prudes. It's just distracting," Alex quips, pressing her lips together.

I want to pat her head since she's at least a sixth of a fathom shorter than me. But I clasp my hands behind my back to remove the temptation. "Distracting?" I push my chest out and shimmy, unable to resist teasing this adorable human.

Alex's face turns bright pink. *Oh my! Now, that is a cute color.*

"Don't do that!" she shrieks.

"Why not? You know, you could just touch them. That would probably lessen the novelty of my naked breasts."

She scowls. "I am not touching your boobs!"

I snicker. "Then we are at an impasse since I don't have any clothing."

With a huff, she stomps to a pair of shorts and a shirt draped over a couple of plastic chairs. "Here!" She shoves them into my hands. "These should be dry by now."

"Are these yours?"

"Yes. I was wearing them this morning when I jumped in the pool to save you."

I can't suppress my wicked grin.

Her eyes narrow. "Why are you looking at me like that?"

I can't help myself. It's too easy. "I'm just picturing you wet," I tease, wiggling my eyebrows.

Alex blushes again. "Just hurry up and change!"

I should be more panicked that I can't remember anything, but something about Alex is soothing, giving me hope that everything will be okay. Besides, I need to remain positive. And what's more positive than having a good time while teasing this adorable human?

The clothes don't fit properly. My physique is more slender and tall than Alex's short and thick one. As a result, the shorts barely cling to my hips while simultaneously being too short for my long legs. The shirt hides my frame with its billowy fit. It doesn't matter. Once I regain my memory, I'll return to the ocean, where I can shed this annoying glamor.

"Better?" I place a hand on my cocked hip.

She nods. "Much better."

I collapse into the chair I was sitting on earlier. "Tell me what happened."

Alex slides into the chair across from me, which is behind a sleek wooden desk. The permanent scowl on her face melts away to a determined line as she recounts the morning's events.

"Are you sure I mentioned my heart?" I ask once she's finished her story.

Alex lifts her chin. "I'm positive."

I steeple my fingers. "Interesting."

She cocks her head. "Why is that?"

"I feel like it's a clue. Don't you?"

Alex's eyebrows scrunch together. "Uh...sure?"

"It's our first lead!" I jump to the edge of my seat. "We are well on our way to solving this mystery."

"Whoa!" Alex shakes her head, nose crinkling. "'Our' and 'we?' Are you counting me in this equation?"

"You helped me once." I offer her a winning smile.

"Wait a second." Alex gets up and begins pacing the

little room. "I didn't sign up for this. Sure, I saved you, but I have a life. I don't have time to be helping a mythical creature recover her memories."

I snort. "Mythical creature?"

"Krakens aren't real!" She throws up her hands.

I shrug. "Are you calling me a liar? You did see me in my true form, you know."

She whirls on me, eyes wide. "And what is up with that? One minute, you're an octo-taur; the next, you're this drop-dead gorgeous woman!"

I bite back a giggle. "First of all, what is an octo-taur? And second of all, you think I'm gorgeous?" I bat my eyelashes.

"That's not the point!" Her voice is loud and shrill.

This situation is spiraling out of control.

I hold up my hands in surrender. "Fine! Okay! I get it. I understand this is a confusing situation for you. But imagine how I feel. I don't remember anything other than that I'm a kraken."

Alex's face softens, and she lets out a long breath. "I'm sorry. I shouldn't be getting so worked up. This is hard for both of us."

I nod in appreciation. I'm glad my honesty seems to have deflected some of her fear. "And to answer your question, we krakens possess ancient magic. It's not much. Just your typical stuff like talking to ocean animals, super strength, immortality, and glamor."

She stares at me, mouth agape. "Did you say 'immortality?'"

"I did."

"Does that mean you're super old or something?"

I close my eyes and try to remember, but it's like being asked the name of someone you've never met or seen before.

It's blank. What if I never remember anything? Will I ever be able to return to the ocean if I don't know anything about myself?

I fight the hopelessness threatening to rear its ugly head by looking into Alex's gorgeous eyes. I'm thankful for her calming effect on me.

"I'm not sure," I admit with a frown. "I seem to have lost all memories of who I am and how I ended up in your pool."

"I'm sorry." Alex's shoulders slump.

"Don't be." I beam at her, hoping it lifts her spirits. For some reason, it's important to me that this human isn't sad. "I am grateful such a kind human found me. I mean, I would have been fine in the water. But my knowledge about humans is that they fear what they don't understand, and based on your reaction, I take it that I'm right."

She raises and drops a shoulder. "We don't even know your kind exists."

"If someone else found me, it could have ended badly for me," I respond, worry gnawing at my stomach.

We share a long silence. I had hoped that whoever was kind enough to make me a soft and safe place to wake up would also know who I am and what I am doing here. Not that I don't appreciate Alex. I do. I just wish she knew more.

Our silence is interrupted by a low, gurgling growl.

Alex quirks an eyebrow. "Was that your stomach?"

I clutch my belly. "I guess it was. I can't remember the last time I ate." I've just discovered the only thing worse than forgetting your name is being hungry because this shit hurts!

"I left you snacks." She gestures to a yellow tube and a rectangle wrapped in wax paper.

"The random objects next to the cot are food?" I ask, mouth agape.

She scoffs. "Yes. A banana and a granola bar."

I stare at her blankly. "I don't know what either of those things are."

Alex hands me the yellow tube. "Here. Try it."

"What's this?" I take the object from her hands.

"A banana. It's a fruit."

"I have never had a banana before." I rotate the banana in my hand. "Or if I have, I don't remember."

Alex smiles. "You should try it. They are my favorite."

Well, if it's her favorite, then it must be good. I grab it by the stem and bite it from the opposite end. I nearly spit it out. It's bitter, tough, and stringy on the outside but mushy and sweet on the inside.

Alex looks at me, wide-eyed and horrified. "You didn't peel it?"

I grimace as the mushy part begins to melt on my tongue. "Peel it?"

"Give it back real quick." She takes the banana from me and removes the thick yellow skin, exposing a pale center before handing it back to me. "Here."

I force myself to swallow the bite already in my mouth. Shivering, I reluctantly take another bite. The second bite is better, but not by much. The sweetness is overwhelming. I gag.

"Okay!" Alex snatches the banana from me. "No throwing up in my office."

"Do you have any fish?" I ask after swallowing the wretched bite of the banana. A wave of nausea twists in my stomach.

She wrinkles her nose. "Why would I carry fish around?

You know what? Don't answer that. We are on an island, so fish are literally all around us."

I perk up. "Will you take me to the fish?"

Alex rolls her eyes. "Why don't you just return to the ocean and catch your own?"

My shoulders sag. "I don't know what to do," I admit. "If I have family or friends, I don't remember them. The ocean is so massive. How would I know where to go? Honestly, the idea of going back to the ocean right now feels terrifying."

She's quiet for several moments, fidgeting with her hair while starting off into space. She must be deep in thought. She finally sighs. "Alright. I will help you out. But just for tonight."

My eyes become misty. "Really?"

"Yes. Just start thinking about what kind of seafood you want."

Alex removes the shark-shaped ornament that keeps her hair off her neck, letting her sun-bleached sandy tresses fall past her shoulders. I sharply inhale as I'm hit with the urge to run my fingers through her hair and comb the snarls. My tentacles stir beneath my glamor, itching to wrap around her thick thighs.

"Hello?" Alex waves a hand before my face, startling me.

"Sorry." I blink rapidly. "What was that?"

"What kind of seafood do you want?" she asks, tapping her foot.

"There are different kinds?"

She holds up her fingers to count the options. "There's your classic Americana seafood. Then there's sushi. And on the opposite side of the island, there's even a place that serves seafood boil."

I scratch my chin. Sushi? I have no idea what any of those things are. "Do any of these places have shrimp?"

"You like shrimp?"

I lean forward. "Yes, and I really want some right now."

She snorts a laugh. "You'll love a seafood boil then. We can get crab legs too."

My mouth starts to water. "Please take me there!"

"Alright. Let me grab my bag and see if we can sneak you out."

"Sneak?"

Alex sighs. I get the impression that she does that a lot.

"Yes. I can't let my staff see you."

My brow creases. "Why? I am in the shape of a human."

"True." She shrugs. "But I still can't let them see you."

I nod, pretending to understand. As long as I don't have to eat another banana, I don't care.

She cracks the door and peers outside. After a few moments, she waves for me to follow her. No one's around as we step out of the room, but as soon as we turn the corner, Alex almost runs into a tall, well-built man with rich sepia skin and long locs to the small of his back.

"I knew it!" He points between me and Alex, a gleeful grin showing off perfectly white and straight teeth.

"Uh...Carter! Hi!" Alex sputters. "I don't know what you are talking about."

"I heard you talking to someone in your office! I figured it was a girl!" He eyes me. "And a hot one, too. What the fuck, Alex? Holding out on me?"

"This isn't what it looks like!" Alex holds up her hands and takes a step back.

He crosses his arms over his broad chest. "Oh yeah? What does it look like?"

Her face becomes bright red. "Whatever. I see you put your shirt back on."

Carter chuckles. "Are you going to introduce me to your friend?"

She looks back and forth between me and Carter, mouth rapidly opening and closing. "This is...uh... Ariel!"

I test the name on my lips. "Ariel. Yes, I'm Ariel." It doesn't feel right, but it will do for now.

Carter raises an eyebrow. "Like the mermaid?"

Alex grimaces. "Yeah. Ariel's parents are big Disney fans."

I interject, "Actually, mermaid names are impossible to pronounce with a human tongue. They speak in clicks and whistles, much like dolphins."

Alex looks at me like I've grown a second head, while Carter laughs. "She's funny!"

"Yeah. Hilarious," Alex says deadpan. "Can I take you up on that offer to finish the paperwork?"

"No problem." Carter winks.

Alex glowers at him before taking my hand in hers, and leading me away. "Let's go."

My tentacles squirm from her touch. I close my eyes and force my limbs to be still. Despite this, I'm still disappointed she drops my hand when we reach something called a 'parking lot' that is full of 'cars.' They look like weird little boats to me. Alex's car is something called a 'moped.'

"Can we see it?" I ask, licking my lips.

Alex hands me a hard plastic hat. "See what?"

"The ocean."

Alex nods as she straddles the moped. "Not only will

we see it on the drive, but the restaurant overlooks the ocean." She motions for me to join her.

I hop on, eager to see my home, even if I'm not ready to be in it yet. "Maybe seeing it will help me remember."

She looks back at me, her eyes soft. "Hey."

"Yes?"

"You're going to be okay. You know that, right?"

My heart swells in my chest and I offer her a tentative smile. "Thanks to you, I will be."

Chapter 3
Alex

I watch from across the little wooden table as Ariel consumes her weight in crab legs and shrimp. It's horrifying. And impressive. Where is she putting it all?

"Are you going to eat that?" She points to my plate of two untouched crab legs.

I slide the plate towards her, full on the too-large portions the restaurant serves. "Uh...no. I'm not."

She beams at me as she takes the food. "Thank you."

"No problem." I take a sip of beer and avert my gaze to look at the rusty sunset over the calm ocean. The constant of the sea always soothes me.

"So where are we?" Ariel asks, around a mouthful of food.

"Crazy Carl's Crustaceans."

She throws back her head and laughs. It's loud, carefree, and charming. "I meant in the world. What is the name of this island?"

"Oh!" I clear my throat. Am I embarrassed by my misunderstanding or is her laugh incredibly adorable? "Sunshine Key."

Ariel sucks the seasoning from her fingers. "Is it always sunny here?"

"Well, the island is technically a part of the Florida Keys, the Sunshine State, so I understand why they would call it that. But honestly, I think the name is a little lame."

"I think it's cute!"

"You would," I mutter into my pint glass.

She nudges me with her foot. "Are you always this grumpy?"

I nearly spit out my beer. I haven't heard someone use that word to describe me since I was a kid. I would find it funny if it weren't so absurd. "Grumpy? Who are you? Snow White?"

"Who is Snow White?" Ariel asks, cocking her head.

"A Disney princess."

She narrows her eyes. "Is she also a mermaid?"

"No. Snow White is just a regular human. Well, kind of. She can sing to animals and make them clean." I shake my head. "Whatever. I can't believe you called me 'grumpy.'"

Ariel shrugs. "It's the perfect word to describe you."

"No, it's not!" I cross my arms over my chest.

She giggles. "You're getting so defensive. It's cute."

My face burns. Other kids always made fun of me for being too much like a boy when I was growing up. 'Cute' was never a word to describe me unless my mom forced me to wear a dress for one of those tacky '90s glamor portraits. The teasing didn't bother me. I am who I am, but it doesn't change the fact that this kind of attention is new to me.

"I'm not getting defensive," I counter. "The last person who called me 'grumpy' was my sister when we were kids. I'm thirty-one now, so that was a long time ago."

"You have a sister?" Ariel leans forward, her eyes

sparkling. "Will I get to meet her? What's her name? Are you close?"

I sigh. "Her name is Avery. We are very close. And you won't meet her if I can help it."

Ariel pouts. "Why not?"

"How would I explain your existence?"

She lifts her shoulders. "Can't you tell her I'm a friend from out of town?"

At that moment, the server approaches our table. He surveys the sea of shellfish carcasses in wonderment. "Do you need to order more?"

Ariel rubs her chin and lets out a contemplative hum. "I think I might be full."

His jaw drops. "You think? You ate enough seafood boil for three people!"

"And it was delicious!" She pats her somehow still flat stomach.

Nate, according to his name tag, stares at Ariel as if she grew a second head.

I clear my throat. "We'll take the check, Nate."

"Yes, of course." He hurries towards the cash register, leaving me to answer Ariel's probing questions.

"Avery and I know almost everything about each other," I explain. "She knows all my friends. Which is just one: Ella."

She twirls a finger in her hair. "I'm a new friend! Technically, we just met today, so that's not even a lie. Why don't you want us to meet?"

I sigh. "I hope that it doesn't take you long to recover your memories so we can both get back to our lives."

Ariel stares into her glass of water with a frown, her shoulders sagging. Her sunny disposition suddenly gloomy. "I'm scared."

"About losing your memories? You'll get them back."

Her gold eyes shimmer with tears. "I'm afraid of what I'll remember. What happened to me that I ended up in the bottom of your pool?"

I hadn't thought of that. I take a long swallow of beer to give myself time to think of a comforting answer. I like to process my emotions alone, so I don't have much practice discussing them. Avery inherited all the 'good at communicating feelings' gene from our father, while I got the 'keep it all inside' from our mother. Because of this, I usually find any excuse to duck out of a conversation as soon as it turns touchy-feely.

"It'll be okay," I offer. I cringe, wanting to punch myself for how dumb that response sounds. What a lame response to someone who is going through a very traumatic event.

Hope sparkles in her eyes. "You'll help me, though, right?"

I hesitate. Saving Ariel from the bottom of the pool? It was my duty as a lifeguard and the right thing to do. Hiding her in my office to keep her safe? It also felt like the right thing to do. Feeding her? Well, I couldn't let the poor kraken go hungry. But to help recover her memories? I'm way out of my depth.

"I don't know, Ariel. How would I even begin to help with that?"

"Be my friend?"

The yearning in her voice hurts my stomach. She wakes up in a strange world that she, at best, has a vague knowledge of, with no personal memories, not even her own name. Not only is she scared and confused, but she must be lonely. My resolve weakens.

"I took you to dinner," I say softly. "That means we're friends now."

Ariel's smile makes my heart flutter. I shift in my seat, hoping that it's just heartburn. Let's not add attraction to this already bonkers situation.

"We just had a delicious meal together. What do we do now?" Ariel asks, flipping her hair over her shoulder.

"Honestly, I'm pretty beat. I would love to go home."

"Alright, then!" Ariel hops up out of her chair. "Let's go."

I freeze. It never occurred to me that she would want to come home with me. But then again, where else is she going to go? She doesn't remember where she lives.

"You want to come home with me?"

It's at that moment Nate approaches with the checks. He drops the tab on the table with a snicker, flicking his eyes between me and Ariel. The heat returns to my cheeks.

"It's not what it looks like." I scramble to pull out my wallet.

He takes my credit card, disappearing from our table as fast as he appeared. "Whatever you say."

Ariel eyes me. "What was that about?"

"Nothing." I avert my gaze. "Just stupid human lingo."

"Tell me," she whines.

I shake my head. I will not explain to Ariel that the server thinks we are about to hook up.

"Come on!" Ariel sings at me. "We can't have secrets between us!"

Nate returns, clicking his tongue. "Secrets, secrets are no fun! Secrets, secrets hurt someone!" He hands over my credit card.

"Do you want a tip or not?" I glare at him. I will still tip him, of course, because I may be 'grumpy,' but I'm not a monster.

He shrugs and saunters off.

"I'll explain later," I murmur as I begrudgingly tip Nate thirty percent. He kept Ariel's plate full, and for that, I appreciate him.

"Will you explain when we get home?"

"Ariel," I begin tentatively. "I don't know if you coming home with me is a good idea."

"Why not?" Her brows knit together. "I'm your friend, right?"

I rub my temples. As an introvert, my home is my curated sanctuary. I'm also a bit of an interior decorating snob. It's important to me that my aesthetic impresses people. And I don't care how gorgeous Ariel is; I don't know if I can forgive her if she doesn't like my design skills.

But I don't have a choice. Ariel is alone, with nowhere to go. Right now, I am her only friend, and like it or not, that means I have to let her judge my home.

"You're right. You are." I rise from the table. "Let's go."

We hop on my moped, and my heart leaps to my throat when Ariel wraps her arms around me and presses her chest against my back. We rode this way to Crazy Carl's Crustaceans, but that was before I knew she was coming home with me.

Now I have Nate's knowing smile in the back of my mind. Even though there's no way we are going to have sex, I can't help but think about it with her perfect human form against me.

It's been a few years since I've been intimate with anyone except my vibrator. Would Ariel even know what to do with my human body? I'm thankful we can't talk or see one another's faces during the ride home. The blush on my cheeks would surely give away my dirty thoughts. Maybe I do need to get laid soon if I'm thinking about sex after the day I just had.

I look at Ariel, wanting to see what she thinks, when we pull up to my house, powder blue and perched up on stilts. The place technically belongs to my parents. It's the home Avery, and I grew up in, but when my parents decided to retire and tour the country in an RV, they didn't want to sell it and see the home they started a family in torn down and two or three smaller residences built in its place.

My parents offered it to my sister first as she is the oldest, but she already owns a house a few streets over. So it went to me. I have to pay utilities, insurance, and property taxes, but I'm grateful I don't have to pay rent or a mortgage.

Ariel gasps when I open the door. "Wow! It's beautiful in here!"

I beam with pride. I took great care in decorating the house with calming blue and green shades. She flops onto the plush couch that happens to be the same shade as her skin when she's in her kraken form.

"This is so comfortable!" Ariel squeals in delight, kicking her feet.

"Do you remember how you slept in the ocean?"

She hums before lighting up. "Under the sand!"

I laugh. "You sleep under the sand? Is that even comfortable?"

She lets out a wistful sigh. "Not like this."

"Just wait until you lay in the guest bed," I say with a smug smile.

"Show me!" Ariel bounces off the couch.

I lead her to the guest room, which used to be Avery's. My old room is still in a shambles as I try to figure out what to do with it. Ariel flings herself onto the plush bed with linens in various shades of purple. The mess to the carefully folded corners and arranged pillows is instantaneous, but I don't mind. Seeing her so enchanted with something as basic as a queen-sized bed warms my heart.

She cuddles a pillow. "How is this even softer?"

I rub my chin. "I wonder if this is your first time not sleeping under the sand."

"You know, I think it is." Her brow creases. "It's crazy that I am remembering this stuff, right?"

"I don't know much about how kraken amnesia would work, but this makes sense. The more you experience things, the more likely you are to know if you have done it before." I snap my fingers when the perfect idea comes to me. "We could expose you to different things and see if it jogs your memory!"

Ariel claps. "That's genius!" She leaps off the bed and flings her arms around me. "I am so glad you saved me!"

My cheeks heat. I'm only five feet tall, but Ariel must be at least six feet tall because her breasts press against my face. I pat her back and struggle out of her embrace. "Let's not get ahead of ourselves. It may not work."

"But it's a start!" She grins, looking radiant.

I open my mouth to agree, but a yawn escapes instead. It's been a long day. I experienced the most physically excruciating rescue of my life, resulting in aching thighs; dealt with the absolute panic of discovering krakens were real; and stressed all day about how I would deal with it. It's just too much for an unadventurous person like me.

Ariel's expression softens. "You must be tired."

"I am." I nod. "If you're okay with it, I'm going to bed."

"Of course." She steps to the side. "Come on in."

I choke on my spit. Sharing a bed with Ariel? I rarely had sleepovers with ex-girlfriends. I can't imagine having one with a tentacled monster. "Oh! I have my own room and bed."

Her bottom lip juts out in a pout.

Did she really expect us to sleep together? Ariel must be really shaken if she's that desperate for a friend. I guess I would be too if I had lost my memories.

I place a comforting hand on her shoulder. "I'll be right across the hall." I point to my bedroom door. "Just knock if you need anything."

Ariel offers me a soft and appreciative smile. "Thank you, Alex. For everything."

"No problem." I turn towards my room, eager to put on my pajamas, and then pause. "Shit!"

Her body stiffens. "What's wrong?"

"You need clothes to sleep in." I can't believe I forgot that Ariel needs pajamas.

She laughs. "No need! I was going to sleep naked."

"You can't!" I sputter.

"Don't you sleep naked?"

"Absolutely not!" I can't stand to be naked for longer than it takes for me to shower.

Ariel shakes her head. "But clothes are so itchy."

"Then I'll make sure you have softer ones. But you can't be naked."

Ariel stares at me. Her eyebrows furrow in a way that I now know means she's thinking. Finally, a small smile curls at the corner of her mouth. "Alright. Give me some clothes to sleep in."

I breathe a sigh of relief. I could not handle a hot chick sleeping naked in my house after everything that happened today. I just don't have the mental energy.

I leave Ariel in the guest room and rifle through my dresser, looking for the most comfortable pajama set I own. I find the silk set my best friend Ella gifted me as a joke for my last birthday. Personally, I prefer flannel, even in the Florida heat. They are just so cozy.

I return to Ariel and pass her the pajamas. "Do these feel soft enough for you?"

"Oh my goddess!" She rubs her face in the silk. "These are wonderful! I can't wait to put them on."

And as if this is some kind of sick joke the universe is playing on me, she pulls her shorts down.

"Whoa!" I cover my eyes. "Wait until I leave the room!"

"But you've already seen me naked once."

I squeeze my eyes shut and turn away. "Doesn't mean I have to keep seeing you naked."

An exhausted sigh escapes from my lips when I close my bedroom door behind me. I drag myself to my ensuite bathroom, where I brush my teeth and conduct my skincare routine. It's a highly self-indulgent act, but applying various creams is soothing after all day in the sun. My eyes are heavy as I hurl myself into my bed. I look forward to a blissful sleep.

Except sleep doesn't come.

Instead, I toss and turn. I keep thinking about the events of the day and the gorgeous woman across the hall in my pajamas. Since I'm not moving anymore, my brain has taken the opportunity to start running a marathon. I'm about to give up and take some melatonin when there's a knock on my door.

I climb out of bed. "Hold on!" I know I should be annoyed that my non-existent sleep has been interrupted, but I'm relieved to have something to do.

When I turn on the light and open the door, I find Ariel fidgeting and scratching herself. Her eyes are wide with fear.

"What's wrong?" I ask with a gasp.

"My skin!" Even in the dim lighting from my bedroom, the red marks from her nails are visible. "It feels like it's on fire!"

I grab her hands to stop her scratching. "Is it the pajamas? Do you have allergies?"

Ariel wrenches herself from my grip and drags her nails over her skin. "I just feel so dry! I need water!"

"Please stop!" I grab her hands once again, squeezing them tightly in mine. I could take her to the ocean, but she needs relief now. "Follow me!"

I pull her into my bathroom. This space was my parents' before mine, and they spent a lot of money and time in the bathroom. They love to take baths together, so the garden tub is large and deep enough for two people. I still haven't used it yet, but it will be perfect for Ariel.

I'm careful when I turn on the faucet. The water can't be hot because it will hurt where she's scratched herself, but I also want the pressure as high as it can go so the tub will fill fast.

"Try not to itch yourself. This shouldn't take long. Go ahead and get undressed."

Ariel trembles as she slides the silk pajamas off her lean body. Her pale skin is a sickly gray, and her full lips are white. I glance away to give her privacy. I wish for the tub to fill faster, but it keeps the same flow speed. Over the roar of the water, I hear her whimper.

"Fuck it!" The tub is only a quarter full, but I can at least get part of her in the water. "Get in the bathtub!"

I assist Ariel into the tub, but as soon as she sits in the water, her legs lengthen and split into six tentacles. I watch, horrified, as she turns from a sickly pale gray to a blue. Webbing grows between her fingers. A low, relieved moan escapes from the back of her throat. *What the fuck is happening?*

She's a kraken again.

I screech. "Did you do that on purpose?"

Ariel's golden eyes shimmer once again. I would be enthralled with their beauty if I wasn't freaking the fuck out. "No. I didn't." She shakes her head." I swear.

My jaw drops. "What happened?"

"When my legs got wet, I turned. I couldn't help it."

Oh shit. This is going to be a problem.

Chapter 4
Ariel

Alex looks at me, her mouth agape and eyes wide in horror. For the first time since meeting her, my cheeks heat up. Does she find my true form frightening? Or worse, disgusting? My tentacles curl in shame.

"I'm sorry," I whisper, hanging my head.

"No. No need to apologize." She holds up her hands. "I'm just thinking about how this creates a new problem."

Of course, it does. I can't be in my true form around anyone other than Alex, nor can I stand to use human glamor for too long without my skin burning. And now we have this new issue where I can't get wet except in private. I am becoming one big inconvenience.

"I should be apologizing. You wouldn't be dealing with this if you hadn't saved me today." My eyes become bleary.

I've disrupted Alex's whole life by asking for her help. She should be sound asleep right now, but instead, she's awake, taking care of me and my problems. I should ask Alex to take me to the ocean. It's big and intimidating, but maybe it won't be so bad when I'm in it. I'm a kraken! I belong in the sea, not some oversized basin.

"Hey!" Alex kneels beside the tub and takes my hand. "Today threw a lot of surprises at me, for sure. But I am here for you. We will figure this out. Together."

I squeeze her hand. I love how small her hands feel in mine. This time, my tentacles twitch with curiosity. They long to wrap around her and hold her tight. I force my tentacles to stop inching towards her. It takes a lot of concentrated effort. It's like they are drawn to her by some sort of supernatural force.

My tentacles' subtle tremors and movements say more about my inner thoughts and feelings than my face ever could. And I'm pretty positive they've never reacted to someone like this. I would remember that. Wouldn't I? Part of me wants to talk to Alex about it, but I am not even sure what it means, so I keep it to myself.

Alex grasps my hand tighter. "Are you okay?"

"Yes. My apologies. Just a little distracted." I force out what I hope is a convincing smile.

"Understandable." She lets go of me and leans over the basin she calls a 'tub' to turn off the faucet. The water is almost overflowing. "Do you need anything else right now?"

"Just a few more moments." I prop my arms over the edge of the tub. "I feel much better already."

"I know you said it wasn't the silk pajamas, but would you like to sleep in something else? What will make you the most comfortable?"

A small smile tugs at the corners of my mouth. Alex's usual crabby exterior has melted away, revealing a kind caretaker. Is this her authentic self, while her prickly attitude is just a front? I long to ask her, but I know she would deny it. It's something I'll have to experience for myself.

"Actually, I was hoping I could stay a kraken for the night."

The idea of being in my human form again makes me want to cry. It's hard to maintain, and I can't imagine doing it while sleeping. "I understand if you don't want me to. I'll do my best to hold my human glamor, but it's honestly quite exhausting."

"Of course." She rubs her chin. "Now that I think about it, as long as you're in my home, you can be a kraken."

I sit up. "Really?"

"Yes." She heads towards the door. "I'll make sure all my blinds are closed. Take your time getting out."

I sink into the tub, relieved, but instantly sit back up when water sloshes onto the floor. The tub is big enough for me to submerge myself, but barely. As long as I stay with Alex, I'll have to soak daily. There has to be a better solution. But first, sleep. Now that I'm no longer agitated and in pain, I'm exhausted. I can't wait to crawl into the soft bed.

Using my tentacles, I carefully heave myself out of the tub, wincing as I soak the floor with water. I panic, grab all the towels off the rack, and begin to mop my mess. Maybe Alex won't be too mad when she returns and sees what I've done to her bathroom if I'm already cleaning up.

"Alright!" Alex shouts as she approaches. "Blinds and curtains are closed." Her mouth drops open when she reaches the doorway and surveys the scene.

I'm keeping myself upright on two of my tentacles while the other four drag already-soaked towels through the puddle outside the bathtub. I offer Alex an apologetic smile, hoping she appreciates my efforts.

"What happened?" she sputters, her face twisting into a grimace.

Oh fuck. Grumpy Alex is back.

I wince. "Well, I may not have been as careful as I could have been getting out of the tub."

"No shit!" Alex sucks in a deep breath. "I appreciate your attempt at cleaning up, but those are my decorative towels."

I laugh. "Decorative towels?" The notion is ridiculous. "Does that mean they are just for looking pretty?"

She scowls. "Yes! That's exactly what they are for. I got them at a really expensive store on the mainland."

I examine the fabric, looking for something that signifies opulence, but I don't find any. As far as I can tell, they are just ordinary white rags. "These are more expensive than normal ones?"

"Yes!" Alex snatches the towels from my tentacles. She squints as she inspects every inch of the fabric before letting out a sigh of relief, apparently happy I've not caused any damage. "I'm sorry for getting so annoyed. I saved up a lot of money to afford this particular brand."

I chew my lip. "And I'm sorry for using the wrong towels. I didn't know there was such a thing as decorative ones."

She shrugs. "I shouldn't have expected you to."

"Why do you want your towels to be just for looking at anyway?"

Alex gets a bright spark in her eyes. "I just really love decorating my space how I like it, you know? In another life, I might have been an interior designer."

"What's an interior designer?"

"It's someone who decorates other people's homes as a career."

"Why aren't you one?"

"I don't know, honestly." Alex hangs her head. "I guess I just never felt good enough. I haven't been to school for it or anything."

"Good enough?" My eyes widen. "Have you seen your home? It's beautiful. Probably better than anyone else's."

Alex's smile is sheepish. "You really think that?"

"Of course." I smile, head held high.

Alex clears her throat, looking down at her feet. "Thank you. I hear that compliment a lot from my sister and best friend, but I always think they are just being nice."

I narrow my eyes. "Do you really think they would lie to you?"

"You know," she chuckles. "Avery would definitely tell me if something sucks, and Ella, while a total sweetheart, is always honest with me."

I smile. "See? You're good. Maybe you can tell me more about what goes into decorating a home. I would love to learn more."

Alex bounces on her toes. "That would be super cool. I'm sure Avery and Ella are sick of listening to me talk about the difference between bone white and soft white."

"Barbarians." I mock gasp.

She snorts as she wrings the towels over the tub. "I'll finish cleaning up in here. Why don't you go to bed? You have a big day tomorrow recovering your first important memory."

"I do?" I ask, head cocking to the side. "What's that?"

Alex grins despite her overdramatic eyeroll. "Your name, of course!"

I wake, much more rested than when I woke on the

makeshift bed in Alex's office at the resort, to soft sunlight straining along the edges of the curtain. I snuggle into the sheets and plush pillows, debating on going back to sleep, but my excitement gets the better of me. Alex said we're going to figure out my name today!

In case she is still asleep, I sneak out of the room. Thankfully, my tentacles make less noise than my human feet. I peek into the hall. Alex's door is still closed, and a pronounced sigh escapes my lips. I hoped she would be awake to give me her plan for helping me remember my name. Plus, I want to see her. She's been so kind to me. I will have to pay her back one day.

I suppress an excited squeal, knowing exactly how I can start to return her kindness—by making breakfast. It won't even come close to repaying what she's done for me, but it's a start. I quietly close the guest room door behind me and creep into the area with the couch.

Sniffing, I search for the scent of food. Something sweet and familiar compels me to a bright white room with red accents. I look around at all the humming machines. Recognition floods back to me.

This room is a galley! I remember! Alex was right. As I experience things, I begin to remember. Now that I think about it, I should have figured it out during dinner last night, especially as I started to recognize things about human culture that Alex didn't have to explain.

My knowledge of human society is limited. Boats are more familiar to me than land-based homes. I get the impression that I have never seen a house up close before last night, let alone been inside one. But I have been on a boat before. I am positive of that. I can't wait to tell Alex.

The familiar scent turns out to be bananas in a large bowl with other fruits. I don't recognize most of them, but the oranges spark a memory of sailors explaining scurvy. I close my eyes, willing the humans in the memory to say my name. I sigh in frustration when they don't.

No matter. There's no point in getting upset. All I can do is push the annoyance aside and focus on what I can control. And what I can control right now is breakfast.

I rifle through the ice box and discover eggs and salmon steaks. Perfection! I find plates, then place two eggs and a salmon steak on each one. I recall that humans love to season their food. I look around the galley and spot canisters with salt and pepper. I give a hearty shake of both over the fish and eggs. My mouth begins to water as the oceanic scent of the salmon wafts to my nose. I don't know how long I will have to wait before eating.

My stomach grumbles so loud that I wouldn't be surprised if I woke Alex. I listen. Nothing. Part of me wishes my rumbles would reach her ears so we can eat breakfast together. I remind myself to be patient. No one likes to be woken before they're ready, even me.

But my resolve lasts all of five minutes. Besides, I don't want breakfast to get too warm. Grabbing each plate, I slither down the hall to her room. I debate knocking but want to surprise her with breakfast in bed, so I turn the knob and enter her room.

Alex's lips are slightly parted, and a curled hand rests against her cheek. My tentacles begin to reach for her, compelled to stroke her face. With a wince, I force them to be still. I need to get them under control, which can be challenging because they sometimes react and move out of instinct. Once I solve the mystery of why they behave this way around her, I will know how to stop them. But I can't keep staring at her, trying to figure it out. I look like a creep.

I clear my throat. "Alex." My voice is low, so I don't startle her.

She doesn't budge.

"Alex." A little louder this time.

Alex emits a tiny snore. Okay. Waking her is going to be more difficult than I thought.

I place my hand on her shoulder and give her a slight shake. "Alex!"

Alex's eyes pop open, staring directly into mine. Success! I take the opportunity to admire the shade of her hazel eyes. I open my mouth to tell her how beautiful they are when she jolts from the bed with an ear-piercing shriek.

I jump with a shout, almost dropping the plates. Why are we screaming?

"What the fuck, Ariel? What are you doing in my room?" Alex's eyes are wild.

I clutch my chest, attempting to calm my racing heart. "I made you breakfast." I tentatively show her the plates with my tentacles.

Alex takes a few deep gulps of air and glares at me. "You should have knocked!"

"I wanted to surprise you!"

"You could have surprised me in the kitchen." She grabs a little black box displaying numbers next to her bed. "I had ten more minutes before my alarm was set to go off. You couldn't have waited?"

I smile once my breathing is finally under control. "But then you wouldn't have breakfast in bed."

Alex scowls. "Well, I'm not in bed anymore after that scare. We might as well eat in the kitchen."

I try not to be disappointed that my plan didn't work as I follow her, attempting to reset my emotions. The good news is that the crease between Alex's brows has dissipated by the time we make it to the galley. She must have calmed down, despite how I unpleasantly woke her. It's the thought that counts. Right?

"Alright!" I set the plates on the counter with pride. "I made us breakfast!"

Alex stares at the food, nose wrinkled. "Is that raw salmon?"

"Yes!" I push out my chest. "And some eggs!"

"Are the eggs cooked, at least?"

My eyes widen. "Should they be cooked?"

"Yes!" Her jaw drops. "You should always cook eggs before you eat them."

"I have eaten eggs uncooked before." I snatch an egg off my plate and pop it in my mouth with a loud crunch. "Isn't it amazing that I can remember that?"

Alex gags. "No!" She coughs. "I mean, yes. It's amazing you remember, but I wish you hadn't."

"Oh." My swallow is loud in my ears. "Is it gross?"

"A little." She winces. "Typically, humans don't eat raw eggs."

I pout. "I didn't know."

"It's okay." She smiles softly. "Now you do."

I eye the plate. "What about the salmon?"

"Well—" Alex gestures towards the salmon. "It's not sushi-grade, so no. It also needs to be cooked."

"Sushi-grade?" There's that weird word again.

"It's a type of food. Lots of raw fish. You would love it."

I do love fish. "Can we go sometime?"

Alex chuckles. "Yes! It will be our celebratory dinner when you recover all your memories."

"That's excellent motivation." I giggle, giddy at the idea of spending more time with Alex.

She begins rifling through the cabinets. "Do you want some coffee?"

"I've never had coffee."

"It's a lot if you've never had it before." She pauses, chewing her lip. "Maybe just a small cup."

I watch as she brews coffee, leaving her breakfast untouched. My stomach sinks.

"Did I ruin breakfast?" I sound pathetic, but I want her to like my food.

Alex looks at me with a small frown. "I'm sorry. I didn't mean to make you feel that way. I don't have time to cook this before work. I'll just have a banana."

I stick my tongue out. Bananas are so gross, and I don't understand how Alex can eat one for breakfast.

"Wait!" The full scope of her statement finally catches up to me. "You have work today?"

Alex sighs. "Unfortunately. I have to open the pool at least, but I'm about to text Carter and see if he can come in early."

"Carter was that really handsome man I met yesterday, right?"

She looks at me in a way I don't recognize, biting the inside of her cheek. "You think he's handsome?"

I giggle. "I mean, I have eyes."

Alex's lips form a thin line and she looks away. Her cheeks are a lovely pink, indicating she's embarrassed or flustered. Usually, she turns this color when I'm teasing her. But her body language screams annoyance. This isn't like the previous times I've made her blush.

My tentacles droop. "Are you upset?"

"No!" she says too sharply.

When I flinch, she sighs. "I'm sorry. I didn't mean to get testy. I just haven't had my coffee yet."

There's something she's not telling me, but I let it go. I haven't told her about my tentacles yet. We both have our secrets. I don't have too long to dwell on our things untold because my stomach gurgles louder than the noisy coffee machine.

Alex laughs. "You can eat your portion of breakfast, you know."

I look at the salmon steak with longing. "Are you sure?"

The machine beeps, and Alex pours the steaming liquid into a small mug. "Here." She hands it to me. "Try it with coffee. You can always add cream and sugar. Please let it cool before you try to drink it."

I wrap my hands around the warm ceramic and inhale the rich aroma. "Thank you. You are too kind."

Alex waves me off as she puts her plate of uneaten food in the fridge. "It's the least I can do."

"What will I do while you're at work?"

Her eyes light up. "I'm glad you asked." She grabs her backpack and pulls out a metallic rectangle. "This is my laptop. I'll show you how to use it. But I'm thinking we can pull up a baby name website, and you can browse it until you figure out your name. I just hope it's nothing too crazy."

I wrinkle my nose. "I don't follow."

"That's okay." Alex laughs. "You'll get the hang of it."

She leads me to the couch in front of another larger rectangle she calls a 'TV.' After a quick tutorial, I understood the laptop enough to navigate the baby-name website. The 'Internet' is a fascinating concept. I try not to ask Alex a billion questions because she's on a time crunch. I chalk it up to some kind of new magic and leave it at that.

I browse the 'A' names while Alex gets ready. I grin when I get to all the variations of 'Alex.'

"Why are you smiling like that?" she asks, returning to the room, dressed in her work uniform. "Did you figure out your name?"

"No. But I found yours!" I point to the screen. "Are you an Alexis or an Alexandra?"

Alex rolls her eyes. "Alexandra. I'm Alexandra Irwin. But I hate it, so I go by 'Alex.'"

I giggle. "Alexandra is cute, but Alex does suit you better."

A blush turns her cheeks pink. "Thanks." She gestures to the TV. "Do you want to watch a movie or a show?"

I stare at her. "I don't know what either of those things are."

"When was the last time you were above water? Do you know what a play is?"

I clap my hands. "I do!"

"It's like that."

"But on this larger laptop?" I look at her, brows creased.

"I'll show you." She grabs a thick yet short plastic stick she calls a 'remote,' and gives me another quick rundown on how to use it. It is also somehow connected to the Internet. I don't understand this magic, but I nod along as if I know.

"Here." Alex navigates to a vibrantly colored image of a woman with a fishtail and bright red hair. "I'll put on The Little Mermaid."

"Is that happy girl supposed to be a mermaid?" I ask with narrowed eyes, staring down the fish woman.

"Yes. That's Ariel."

"Uh...that's not what mermaids look like."

"What do they..." She shakes her head. "Never mind. I can't get into it now. Watch Disney movies and browse baby names. I'll be back soon. Raid the fridge and pantry if you get hungry."

With a wave, Alex exits her house, leaving me alone with an impossibly long list of baby names and a completely inaccurate version of a mermaid. I sip my coffee and spit it back into the mug. It tastes like sludge.

After finishing The Little Mermaid and a movie about a girl who finds a prince via a glass slipper, both of which made me cry due to their hopeless romanticism, I finally make it to the 'M's. My heart picks up speed. Something feels right about that letter. My eyes dart down the page. I can't scroll fast enough.

"Marilyn," I mutter to myself. Close, but not quite it. "Marina." I clench my teeth. Almost there.

I gasp when I read the next name. I found it. I found my name! Memories of a gnarled sailor, mermaids, kelpies, and other krakens using my name flash in my mind. I grasp at them, desperate for more details about them, about me. But nothing comes. I bury my face in my hands and cry over my amnesia for the first time since I woke up in Alex's office. Partly in relief and partly in mourning for myself and those who know me. Do they miss me? Are they looking for me?

The television begins to autoplay another princess movie, this time about one who pricks her finger and falls into a deep sleep. I barely pay attention to it. I slither around the house, eager for Alex to be home so I can tell her the news.

As the credits roll on Sleeping Beauty, the door opens, revealing Alex. She takes one look at me and frowns.

"Are you okay?"

I rush to her, taking her hands in mine. Touching her soothes my anxious mind. "I remember my name."

Her eyes sparkle. "What is it?"
"Maris! My name is Maris!"

Chapter 5
Alex

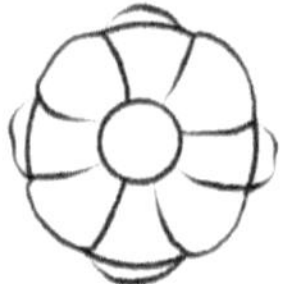

"Maris." I test the name on my tongue. It's perfect for the kraken. It's beautiful, just like her.

I shake that thought away. I can't get caught up in Maris's beauty, not when we have reached a breakthrough. I can't do what I did today: stew over her comment about Carter being handsome. I hate that it bothered me so much. She is an unattainable mythical creature. Carter looks more like a Greek god than anyone I know. Of course she would be into him. And now that I think about it, why would she even be into humans?

Maris's cheeks darken. If I didn't know any better, I would say she's blushing.

"In a way, it's like hearing my name for the first time."

My chest swells. I'm the first person to say her name aloud since she lost her memories. It's remarkably... intimate. "Did you remember anything else?"

"Yes!" Her voice rises in pitch. "I got flashes of what I assume are friends and family. But no concrete details about them or myself."

"That's a start." I nod, pleased with how much progress

she's made. I can't believe the baby name website idea worked. Way to go, me! "I was thinking on my commute that maybe we should go to the beach tonight and see what you can remember."

"You mean I get to go in the ocean?" Maris's tentacles begin to writhe in excitement.

I chuckle. "Yes. But not until night because I don't want anyone seeing your kraken form."

"That makes sense." She chews her lip. "What should we do until then?"

"I'm starved," I admit. "I would love to eat something."

"That's what you get for only eating a banana for breakfast," she huffs. "You should have eaten the food I prepared you."

"Wipe that smug look off your face." I scowl. "I'm not normally this hungry."

She scoffs. "My statement still stands. You know I'm right."

"Whatever. Let's eat. Then maybe we can get you an outfit for parading around the island in human glamor instead of wearing my clothes that are somehow both too big and too short on you."

"That sounds like fun!"

I smile. "I agree. Now what do you want to eat?"

Maris doesn't hesitate. "Fish!"

I sigh. Of course, she wants fish. She's a fucking sea creature. "Do you want the other salmon steak I didn't eat this morning?"

"But that's yours!" Her jaw drops in disbelief.

"Well, it's yours now. I'll have a chicken salad sandwich." I pull the salmon out of the fridge. "Do you want it cooked?"

"No!" She licks her lips. "I'll take it raw."

I place a few eggs on her plate and slide it across the counter. Maris snatches the food and begins shoveling it in her mouth with the same gusto she ate the seafood boil last night. She must have been hungry. I'm glad I buy eggs in bulk because this kraken is devouring them.

I avoid watching Maris consume her meal as I prepare my sandwich. She may be gorgeous, but her table manners are horrendous. She has licked the plate clean by the time I finish making my meal.

"Are you still hungry?" I try to keep my tone neutral, but I think a little bit of awe still slipped out. How does she do it?

"Maybe a little," she admits, looking at the floor.

I rummage through my cabinets, pull out several stacked tuna cans, and hand them to her. "Here."

Maris squints, looking between me and the cans. "This is fish?"

"Yes." I take a can from her and demonstrate how to open the tab before handing her a fork. "That's how you open them, and I would prefer you use a fork. I don't want tuna juice everywhere."

"Affirmative." Maris sticks her fork in the meat and scoops a large bite into her mouth. Her face twists as she chews. "What in the goddess's blue ocean is this?"

"It's tuna." The reply slips from my lips sounding more like a question than an answer.

"It tastes...dead."

"Of course. That's because it is dead." I wave to the empty plate. "So was the salmon and all the shellfish you ate last night."

Maris grimaces. "But this tastes extra dead."

I laugh. "That's a good way to describe it. It's been dead

for a while and super overcooked." I watch as she takes another bite. "But you don't seem to mind."

Maris swallows. "It sucks, but it's better than that banana."

"And for that—" I snatch a banana off the counter. "I am going to eat another one with my lunch."

She wrinkles her nose. "Gross."

I take my food into the living room and plop onto the sofa. "Not as gross as unseasoned canned tuna."

Maris sits down next to me and nudges me with her shoulder. "What're we doing on the couch?"

I gesture to the TV. "I figured we could watch a movie while we eat. I need some decompression time, if that's okay?"

She nods. "Of course. I've been watching these princess films all day."

I finally look at what's currently playing and wiggle with excitement—we're barely ten minutes into Beauty and the Beast.

"Oh!" I grab the remote and turn up the volume. "This one is my favorite!"

Maris grins. "Then I'm excited to watch it."

We eat lunch as Belle falls in love with the Beast. I sing along, off-key, to all the songs, and Maris attempts to harmonize with me by humming. Surprisingly, spending this domestic time with her feels natural, like we've known each other for years rather than just a day.

I stiffen when one of her tentacles wraps around my calf. Her touch is velvety and warm, not slimy and cold like I'd imagined. I relax into her touch. I shouldn't be this comfortable with a tentacle wrapped around my leg, but I am. Is it because Maris and I are becoming friends? I haven't made a new friend in so long; I forgot what that feels like.

"Shit!" Maris breathes. She releases her grip. "I'm so sorry. Sometimes, they have a mind of their own."

"I—" My face flushes. Maris and I were touching unprompted, even if she didn't mean it. And I liked it. "It's okay. I didn't even notice." The lie is sour on my tongue, but she's embarrassed, and I don't want her to be.

"Really?" She fidgets with an empty tuna can, refusing to look at me.

"It's fine, I promise." I shift in my seat.

Maris scoots away from me, putting a little extra distance between us, and I fight the disappointment that swoops low in my stomach. We continue watching the movie in relative silence until Belle cries over the Beast. Then Maris bursts into tears.

"She loves him!" she wails. "And now he's dead!"

"Uh..." What am I supposed to do? I haven't seen anyone cry over Beauty and Beast since I was a little kid and Avery and I watched it for the first time. But even then, Avery didn't weep like Maris.

She looks at me, tears streaming down her cheeks. "Please tell me there's a happy ending! I don't think my heart could take it if he stays dead. Does the power of love save him?"

"Maris," I say in what I hope is a soothing voice, pointing to the screen. "I need you to calm down and watch."

Sniffling, she looks back at the television just before the Beast turns into Prince Adam. A deep frown tugs the corners of her full lips downward.

"Did you not like that?" I ask as Belle, Prince Adam, and all the staff dance around the revitalized castle.

Maris wipes the tears from her cheeks. "I'm happy he lived. But I wish he had stayed a beast."

I laugh. "You aren't the only one who feels that way. There are entire books and fan fiction written on that concept."

"How do you feel about the ending? Do you wish he had turned into a human?" She chews her lip as she looks at me, leaning forward.

I hesitate. The entire point of the movie was for the Beast to turn back into a human. Why does Maris care so much? I fight the urge to slap a hand to my forehead. I am an idiot for not realizing it sooner. Is she self-conscious about her kraken shape?

"I think what's important is that Belle is happy," I try to explain carefully. "And she fell for him as the Beast, so I guess it doesn't matter to me."

Maris nods, her eyes holding mine. "You're right. The princess's happiness is all that matters."

After I change into a button-up shirt and a pair of Bermuda shorts, I loan Maris a similar outfit for her human form. While the combination gives me the androgynous figure I desire, it is ill-fitting on her.

Maris prefers to be naked, so flowy dresses and skirts should make her the most comfortable. I'm taking her to Deanna's Delightful Dresses, Ella's favorite boutique in town. On the ride there, I roll my eyes to myself. The business owners on Sunshine Key really love their alliteration, don't they?

When we arrive at the boutique, Maris hops off the back of my moped and emits a delighted squeal, gesturing to the floral dresses in the window display. "I get to wear these?"

I can't help the indulgent grin I give her. "Yes. I figure two or three will suffice for your time here."

Maris dashes into the store, leaving me on the curb. I would have done this last night if all it took was cutesy outfits to get her excited about wearing clothes. When I enter the shop, Maris is already loading dresses into her arms while an exasperated sales clerk watches.

"Maris." I place a hand on her arm to grab her attention. "Do you know your size?"

She stares at me, cocking her head.

"She's grabbed various sizes," the sales clerk offers. "I can take her measurements."

"Thank you...uhh..."

"Sam." Her smile is dazzling.

"Thank you, Sam." I relax my shoulders. "That would be helpful."

Maris pouts. "But I like these dresses."

I take the garments from her arms. "I am sure the shop has all of them in your size." I nod towards Sam. "Get measured. These dresses will be here for you."

As Sam measures Maris, I carefully rack the garments. I don't want to leave a mess in our wake. Usually, I would eye the price tags, stressing over how much this shopping excursion will cost. But instead, I imagine each dress on Maris. She would look stunning in any of them.

I'm jolted out of my fantasy dress montage by Maris squalling at me that she's a size medium. Together, we dig through the racks. I lean towards blues and greens, not only because they are my favorite colors but because they would complement her golden eyes. Meanwhile, Maris has picked various shades of pink.

"I'm surprised." I nod towards the garments in her arms.

"Why?" she asks, rubbing the fabric of a dress between her fingers.

"They're all pink."

She beams. "I love pink! Red light is the first to filter as you go deeper into the ocean, so I don't see it often." Maris snaps her fingers. "Hey! I just remembered that about myself!"

I glance at Sam to see if she's listening to this bizarre conversation, but she appears to be politely ignoring us, waiting for the moment we need her.

"That's excellent," I whisper, leaning close to Maris. "But keep the talk about living in the ocean and not having your memories quiet."

She sucks in a breath and glances around. "Sorry."

"It's okay." I adjust the pile of dresses in my arms. "I don't think I can hold anymore. Should you start trying stuff on?"

As if the words activated her hearing, Sam appears next to us. "The dressing rooms are this way."

She leads Maris to a row of rooms with thick curtains in the doorways for privacy. Sam hangs the dresses we picked out on a rolling clothing rack.

"I'll hand you one dress at a time to prevent clutter in the dressing room," she explains with a polite smile. "Let me know if you need assistance getting in or out of the garments."

Maris skips behind a curtain, clutching a teal dress in her hands.

For about an hour, my daydream montage of Maris trying on various outfits comes to life. She disappears behind the curtain, giggles as she dresses, and then exits the dressing room with a flourish, twirling and voguing in each dress. Sam and I clap in approval or shake our heads in dislike, depending on how flattering each dress is on her lithe frame.

She walks out in a baby blue maxi dress, and my cheeks hurt from smiling. When was the last time I had this much fun?

My life is pretty routine. I wake up, go to work, hit the gym, go home. My weekends include homemaking and occasionally having dinner and drinks with Avery and Ella. I'm content with my life, but time with Maris has shaken things up. And, surprisingly, I'm not mad about it. I've always struggled with mixing up my patterns, but with her, it's easy.

"Alex?" Maris interrupts my thoughts. "What do you think?"

I smile at her. "It's lovely."

"It's the last dress," Sam points out. "She's tried on every dress in her size."

"Really?" Maris twirls. "I've been having so much fun!"

I look at the rack of garments. "Do you think you can narrow it down to five?"

"Hmmm." She chews her lip. "You pick! Which are your favorites?"

I try to hide my surprise. No one has ever trusted me to style them before, probably because I dress like a frat boy most of the time. But now, the most beautiful woman I've ever seen, has asked me to choose her outfits. A thrill shivers down my spine.

"Uh..." I stammer, still in shock at her question. "Yeah."

I approach the rack and take my time going through the approved dresses. With great care, I consider which dresses made her light up the most. I pick a blue, a seafoam, a floral, and two pink dresses. Maris blushes when I show her my choices. My heart pitter-patters at the adorable pink color her cheeks turn.

But not as adorable as the dark blue they turn when she's in her kraken form.

"These are perfect!" she breathes.

I beam with pride. "I'm glad you like my picks."

Maris grabs the one that happens to be my favorite shade of blue. "I want to wear this one right now." She looks at Sam. "Can I do that?"

"Of course!" Sam smiles, probably pleased with the decent commission she's about to earn. "Let me grab the tag, and I'll ring you up."

Maris changes while I make the purchases. I thank Sam for her help, genuinely appreciative of her patience.

"No problem." She giggles. "You and your girlfriend are so cute."

"No!" I shout, stunned by Sam's assumption. Heat flushes my face and neck. "I mean—" I lower my voice. "She's not my girlfriend."

She chuckles. "My apologies."

I glare at her as she hands me the receipt. Maybe if I act outraged at her suggestion, my heart will calm down. The idea of Maris and I dating is absurd. She's a legendary sea monster, and a gorgeous one at that. I'm sure she has an equally stunning kraken partner back in the ocean she just can't remember right now.

I'm grateful my moped isn't the best environment for chatting. My pensive mood wouldn't make me a sparkling conversationalist at the moment. Not only am I still embarrassed by the store clerk calling Maris my girlfriend, but there's a part of me that will miss her when she recovers her memories and returns to the sea. I'm such a selfish prick.

Thankfully, when we pull into my driveway, Maris is ready to fill the silence by thanking me for all I've done for her.

"It's the least I can do," I reply. And I mean it. Poor Maris probably feels so lost and confused right now. She needs a friend.

"Seriously, Alex." She places a hand on my shoulder when we reach the top of the stairs. "It means a lot. I couldn't do this alone."

We hold each other's gaze, maybe longer than we should. There are so many things I want to say to her. I should be the one to thank her for bringing some excitement into my life and opening my eyes to the fact that there are mystical things in the world. I will never be the same.

I open my mouth to say all of this when my front door flings open. *What the fuck?* Is my house acting on its own will now? I scream and nearly stumble down the steps, but Maris catches my arm.

"Where the fuck have you been?"

I recover from an almost disastrous fall down the stairs. When I stand up, I am astounded to see my sister.

"Avery?" My mouth flaps open.

What is she doing here, and how did she get in my house?

As if reading my mind, Avery dangles a key in my face. "I have a spare key, remember?"

"Oh."

"Oh?" She crosses her arms over her chest. "You haven't replied to any of my texts since the day before yesterday, so I show up at your house to check on you, and you roll up with a certified hottie? What the hell, Alex?"

I look between Avery and Maris. How am I going to explain this to Avery? I suck in a deep breath. I'm fucked.

Chapter 6
Maris

"What the hell, Alex?" Avery repeats.

Alex's mouth opens and closes.

This is bad. If she doesn't respond soon, Avery will start making assumptions, which I've learned makes Alex very uncomfortable, especially regarding me. I need to step in.

"Hi!" I wave at Avery. "My name is Maris."

Avery looks at me with familiar hazel eyes. She looks a lot like Alex, except her hair brushes her shoulders in a wavy bob, and she has darker lashes as if she's wearing paint or something on them to draw attention to her eyes. I force a smile, hiding the urge to squirm under her scrutinizing gaze. Just when I think she's about to return to berating Alex, a large grin lights up her face.

"Avery!" She pulls me in for a tight hug. "Nice to meet you. Are you fucking my sister?"

Alex coughs, turning bright red. "Avery!"

My tentacles twitch under my glamor, but I smile through it. It's time to do my favorite thing. Tease Alex.

"Unfortunately, no."

"'Unfortunately?'" Alex sputters. "Maris!"

Avery throws back her head and laughs. "You're hilarious! I like you."

"This isn't funny!" Alex glares at us.

"It absolutely is!" Avery grins wide. "But the real question is, why haven't you slept with your new girlfriend?"

"She's not my girlfriend!" Alex's voice is shrill.

"Bullshit!"

As amusing as it is to fluster Alex, I decide to put her out of her misery. "I'm not her girlfriend. We're just friends."

Alex sighs in relief, grateful for my intervention. "Yeah! Just friends."

"Then why haven't you responded to my messages?" Avery huffs. "We never go longer than like twelve hours without talking."

Once again, Alex flounders, searching for a way around the truth.

"Alex rescued me at the pool yesterday, and we became fast friends. Turns out, saving someone's life is a great bonding experience." It's not a lie. I'm just leaving out the fact I'm a kraken.

Avery waggles her eyebrows. "I'm impressed. Alex hasn't made a friend since kindergarten. You must be pretty cool."

"Yeah," Alex agrees. "Maris is pretty cool." She turns her signature glare to Avery. "Now that we've established I'm not fucking anyone, why did you feel entitled to show up to my house?"

"Do you know how many times I've tried messaging and calling you? Your calls have been going straight to voicemail. I got worried. I'm assuming now it's either because you have it turned off or on do not disturb."

Alex fishes her phone out of her pocket and looks at the

screen, horrified. "Oh shit! Avery, I'm so sorry. I've been so caught up in things since the rescue that I forgot to take it off do not disturb."

Avery gives me a long look, scanning me from head to toe, a sly grin curving her lips. "I can see why."

Alex's eyes narrow. "What do you mean by that?"

"Nothing!" She holds up her hands in surrender. "Have you two eaten dinner yet? I'm starved!"

"Me too!" I perk up. "Can we have fish?"

"Wait a second!" Alex's eyes dart between me and Avery. "What makes you think we're all eating dinner together?"

Avery giggles. "Why are you freaking out? Are you worried I'm going to wife up your new friend?" She wraps her arm around my shoulders and leans into me.

Alex glares at Avery. "No. I just wasn't expecting you. I barely know what to prepare for me and Maris."

"Good thing I can always order us some pizza." She pulls out her phone. "Peter's Perfect Pizza sound good?"

"Pizza." I test the word, partly to see if I can remember what the heck a pizza is and partly because I like the way the word buzzes in my mouth. "What is a pizza?" I ask with a smile.

Avery drops her arm from around my shoulder and steps back, stunned. "How do you not know what pizza is?"

"Maris isn't from around here," Alex interjects, nearly stumbling over the words to get them out quickly.

"Oh!" Avery rubs her chin. "I thought I heard an accent. Where are you from?"

"Europe!" Alex claps her hands, changing the subject. "Let's order pizza! Maris, I have plenty of tuna if you don't like it."

After Avery orders our dinner, she rummages through a cabinet in Alex's living room, looking for board games. I am familiar with some games sailors used to play, such as dominos, checkers, or cards. A memory of the gnarled sailor returns. This time, he's teaching me to play cribbage.

His details are fuzzy at first, but come roaring back all at once with a crash. His name was Thomas Booth, and he was the captain of the *Stella Maris*, a pirate ship known for intercepting the spice trade. I rescued him from a boat wreck when he was a young sailor in the Royal Navy before he defected to piracy. When he eventually became captain of his own boat, he named it after me. We were best friends until he died of old age in the arms of his first mate and long-time lover.

The recollection is a gut punch, leaving me breathless. The weight of missing Thomas is heavy, smothering the happiness and hope from learning my name and meeting someone as amazing as Alex. The wound of remembering him is raw and painful. I fight back tears. I can't succumb to grief in front of Alex and Avery.

"Are you okay?" Avery asks.

I can't see her expression through my gathering tears, but her tone is soft and full of concern.

"Yeah." I wipe my eyes. "I once had a friend who loved playing games, especially cribbage."

"A friend?" Alex approaches and puts a hand on my shoulder. Her touch instantly soothes me, grounding me in the moment rather than drifting in the painful past. "You remember a friend?"

"I do. Thomas."

A smile lights up Alex's face. "This is wonderful."

Avery gasps. "Alex! What the fuck? She's hurting. Also, why are you talking about her memory?"

"Right." Alex grabs my hand. "Will you excuse us for a minute?"

"But—"

Alex doesn't let Avery finish her thought and begins dragging me down the hall to her bedroom.

She closes the door behind us. "Who is Thomas? What triggered a memory?"

When Alex drops my hand, the emptiness of losing Thomas returns. Instead of answering her, I have a question of my own. "Can you hold me?"

Her eyes widen, and she opens her mouth as if to say something, but snaps it closed with a disbelieving head shake. My stomach drops. She's going to reject me, and I can't handle it if she does. Something deep inside me needs Alex and her touch.

"Please?" I whisper.

Alex's face softens, and she opens her arms. "Come here."

I lean into her, and she envelops me. Alex may be shorter than me, but it doesn't diminish how comforting and safe it feels to be in her arms. Her body is soft against mine, and the fresh scent of her botanical lotion is sweet in my nose. I suck in deep breaths, my anguish melting away in her embrace. Being this close to Alex dulls the pain.

"Are you going to be okay?" Alex murmurs against my chest.

"I am now." I fight the urge to run my fingers through her hair.

She pulls back just enough to look me in the eyes. "What happened?"

"Seeing all those games reminded me of the ones I learned to play with human sailors." I let out a shaky breath.

"And then I remembered Thomas. He was my best friend."

"Well, that's great. Maybe we can find Thomas, and he can help..." She pauses. "Wait. 'Was?'"

I droop my head and shoulders. "He passed away."

Alex pulls me against her. "I'm sorry, Maris."

"It happened a long time ago." My bottom lip trembles. "I would be fine, but when the memories came flooding back, it felt like reopening a wound."

She squeezes me. "I can only imagine. Do you want to tell me about Thomas?"

I reluctantly step back. "Not right now. We should rejoin your sister."

"Are you sure?"

I smile, endlessly thankful for her kindness. "I feel better."

Her eyebrows pinch. "We can stay in here longer if you need it."

For a moment, I consider taking her up on the offer. But maybe it's best if I have a distraction. I don't need to dwell in my grief. Besides, I don't want to worry Alex.

I shake my head. "I'm good, I promise."

Alex's eyes search mine before finally softening. "Alright. If you're ready, let's get back out there."

Avery eyes us when we reenter the room but doesn't say anything, probably because I catch Alex shooting her a stern look. Together with Avery, we select a deck of cards and plastic chips to play Poker. Avery explains the game's rules, and I'm thankful I catch on to gameplay quickly. Just as Alex finishes shuffling the deck of cards, there's a knock on the door.

"Pizza!" Avery jumps from her seat and skips to the door. She collects several shallow boxes from a young man and then plops them on the table. The smell is greasy yet intoxicating. My mouth begins to water.

My jaw drops when Alex opens the lid to reveal the pizza. The flat disc is unlike anything I've seen before. I'm amazed by the melty cheese and how it stretches when Alex pulls a slice for me and places it on a plate.

"Let me know if you like it," she says, leaning forward to watch me take a bite.

What if it's as bad as some of the other human foods I have tried? I take a tentative nibble of pizza.

Oh my! It's delicious!

I've never tasted anything so savory and complex. I wolf down another bite, desperate to have that flavor on my tongue again.

"Whoa!" Avery's jaw drops. "That was a big bite. I assume you like the pizza?"

I nod and shove the rest of the slice in my mouth. Even the bready crust is fantastic.

"Oh my god! Don't choke!"

Alex plops another slice onto my plate. "Don't worry. She's just an enthusiastic eater."

"What's that supposed to mean?" I ask around a mouthful of food.

Alex snickers. "You know exactly what I mean. You're a little messy."

I swallow before barking a laugh. "I'm sorry. I'm just so hungry."

"It's alright," she says with an amused smile. "Try to slow down so you can fully enjoy it."

I attempt to eat my second slice with less gusto. But the pizza is so tasty that I still devour it before Alex and Avery even finish their first piece.

Alex picks up the cards. "What should we bet with?"

"Sailors used to gamble with gold." I shrug as I reach for another serving of pizza.

"Let's have a more casual night," Alex suggests. "Gambling money is messy."

Avery perks up. "What about truth or dare?"

"How would that even work?"

"Whoever has the most chips at the end of the night gets to force the other two players to choose between a truth or a dare."

I waggle my eyebrows. "I've never played, but it sounds scandalous."

"It could be." Avery begins to split the chips between us. "Do we all agree?"

Alex crosses her arms over her chest with a frown at Avery. "I don't trust you."

"Oh, come on!" Avery bats her eyelashes. "You don't trust your big sis?"

"Not at all," Alex deadpans.

Avery clutches her hand over her chest. "I'm hurt."

I giggle. "You're breaking her heart."

"Yeah, Alex. I may never recover from this."

Alex scowls. "I knew the two of you together would be trouble."

Avery chuckles. "It's called 'having fun.' You should try it sometime."

"Fine." Alex sighs. "We can play for truth or dare. Just promise you won't have us do anything weird if you win."

"Hell yeah!" Avery pumps her fist in the air. "Who knew a little bullying would go so far?"

"Whatever." Alex begins dealing the cards. "Let's get this over with."

Time flies by. I eat the entirety of a pizza while we play several rounds of Poker. I learn quickly that Alex's tell is a twitch in the corner of her mouth. It's too easy to call her bluffs. Meanwhile, Avery's face remains neutral, and she dominates us the entire night.

It reminds me of playing games with Thomas and his crew. There's laughter, arguments, and exclamations of victory. My cheeks hurt from smiling, and I'm having so much fun that I'm able to ignore the dull itch for water.

By the time we finish our last round, the majority of the chips are in front of Avery. She beams with pride as she counts them out loud to rub her victory in our faces.

"How does it feel to be a couple of losers?" She laughs.

I grin. "I had so much fun that I don't even care that I lost."

Alex rolls her eyes, though I can tell she's fighting back a smile. "I'm annoyed you won."

Avery chuckles. "Are you scared to play truth or dare?"

"Honestly, yes. I still don't trust you." She glowers.

Avery turns to me. "What about you? Nervous?"

"I'm excited," I admit, fidgeting in my seat. "I've never played truth or dare."

"I'm pleased this will be your first experience." Avery rubs her hands together. "I'll ask Alex first so you can observe." She turns to her sister. "Truth or dare?"

Alex sighs. "Truth."

Avery frowns. "Really?"

"Yes."

"You're so boring," Avery scoffs, rolling her eyes.

"Cry me a river."

Avery laughs. "Alright. I can still make this fun." She looks between me and Alex with a cunning smile. "Do you think Maris is attractive?"

My heart skips a beat. I wasn't expecting something like this. My emotions switch between hope and despair. Will

Alex be judging me based on my human or my kraken form? I want to know what she thinks of me, but I don't think I can handle the disappointment if she finds me unattractive, especially without my glamor.

I don't know why it matters to me that she considers me beautiful as a kraken. But it's the same reason my tentacles long to wrap around her. I'm so close to the answer. The answer is on the tip of my tongue, but I can't quite remember.

Alex turns bright red. "I don't want to answer that."

"Cry me a river," Avery sing songs. "You lost. Pony up, bitch."

"You know I can't lie!"

"Exactly." Avery's grin reminds me of a shark.

Alex won't look at me.

I hold my breath and shift in my seat, my tentacles writhing beneath my glamor. I want to scream at her to get it over with and tell me she finds me ugly. My skin itches, and I fight the urge to claw at it, suddenly desperate to be out of this human skin.

Alex's confession is barely audible. "I think she's the most beautiful creature I've ever seen."

Blood rushes to my head, and the room spins as I attempt to process what she said.

"Okay. Calling her 'creature' is a little creepy, but I knew it!" Avery claps. "I mean, how could you not? Maris is stunning. I'm so glad I got you to—"

"All of me?" I blurt, interrupting Avery's moment of triumph. I have to know. Does she find this mask beautiful or the real me? I don't care that Avery's quizzical gaze bounces between us.

The silence is heavy as I await Alex's answer. When

she finally looks at me, her hazel eyes shine with determination. It takes my breath away.

"Yes. All of you."

Heat flushes my skin. I'm at a loss. I was convinced Alex could never find the real me attractive. Do I thank her? Do I tell her how beautiful I think she is? Do I take her into my tentacles and hold her close?

I do none of those things. Instead, I look away like a coward, unable to confront the twisting emotions in my stomach. Relief, hope, and want fight to consume me. I can't allow this to rule me. Humans can recognize beauty without having any desire behind it. Thomas found me stunning but was not interested in the female form.

Avery steeples her fingers together with a maniacal laugh. She looks like a villain from one of the Disney movies I watched. "Well, Maris. What will it be? Truth or dare?"

A million thoughts rush through my mind. If I pick 'truth,' she might ask me how I feel about Alex. I don't want to make either of us more uncomfortable than we already are, but 'dare' seemed to freak Alex out. What kind of action would Avery dare me to do? Besides, I want to be brave and impress Alex.

I square my shoulders. "Dare!"

That cunning shark smile returns. "Excellent. Maris, I dare you to kiss Alex."

Alex leaps from her chair, clattering her short stack of poker chips. "Whoa! Avery! What the fuck?"

I'm stunned, frozen in place over Avery's challenge. Kiss Alex? My heart soars. I would die to feel her lips against mine. But based on her reaction, she doesn't want the same, confirming my fear that she doesn't want me.

Avery scoffs. "Are you telling me you don't want to kiss the most beautiful woman you've ever seen?"

"It's not that. I just..." Alex throws her hands in the air. "What if Maris doesn't want to?"

Avery turns to me. "What about it, Maris? Are you going to back down from your dare? Don't you think my sister is cute?"

I clench my jaw. If only Avery knew how much I want this. I consider Alex's response. She's worried about me not desiring the kiss? How could she ever think that? Does this mean she wants it, too? Going through with this kiss is risky. It could alter our friendship for the worse. But now that Avery presented the idea of kissing Alex, I want nothing more.

I bite my lip. "Only if Alex consents," I respond.

Avery looks at Alex with raised brows. "Well?"

"I am not kissing someone in front of my sister." Alex scrunches her nose. "It's weird."

Avery blanches. "On second thought, wait until I go to bed to kiss."

"Who says we are going to kiss at all?" Alex blanches.

"Keeping it mysterious, I see." Avery winks. "Well, speaking of bed. I am tired. I call dibs on the guest room!"

"Hell no!" Alex points towards the front door. "Go home!"

Avery pouts. "But we haven't had a sleepover in forever. Besides, would you really make your sister walk home in the dark?"

I nod. "She has a point. It could be dangerous out there."

Alex rolls her eyes. "She's fucking with me. She only lives a half mile away."

"But that doesn't stop me from being right." Avery clasps her hands together as if in prayer. "Please! Come on,

Alex! I don't work tomorrow, and I want to hang out with my new friend."

My heart swells. "You consider us friends?"

"Of course!" She beams.

I can't help the huge grin that spread across my face. Another new friend? I'll take it. Especially after remembering the loss of my best friend.

Alex looks at me, puzzled, before her expression softens. "Fine. You can stay, Avery."

Avery and I both let out excited squeals.

"Don't make me regret this," Alex warns, jabbing a finger at Avery.

"Whatever do you mean?" Avery asks, batting her eyelashes.

"Whatever."

"Love you, little sis," Avery sings as she saunters down the hallway to the guest room.

"No way! If you're going to stay here, you're sleeping on the couch."

But Avery doesn't turn around. "But I'm old, and I have a bad back."

"You're only thirty-five!"

"Respect your elders." Avery pauses before entering the guest room. "Good night, Maris. It was lovely meeting you. I hope we have tons of fun together tomorrow."

A giddy rush of excitement bubbles out of me in the form of a giggle. "I look forward to it."

"See you tomorrow," she says before shutting the guest room door behind her and leaving Alex and me alone.

Alex clears her throat. "Sorry about my sister."

My eyebrows scrunch together. "Why? I really enjoyed her company."

"I mean about the whole 'dare' thing."

"Oh." My shoulders sag, remembering that Alex rejected my kiss. "I shouldn't have even entertained the idea. We made you uncomfortable and—"

"It's okay. I…" She looks away, cheeks flushing pink. "It's just been a while since I kissed someone."

Is that why Alex didn't want to kiss me? She's nervous?

I move closer to Alex. "That's okay. I can't remember the last time I kissed someone."

Alex's eyes sparkle, the corner of her perfect mouth upturning. "You can't remember anything. It doesn't count."

"Sure it does. If we kissed, it would be like my first time. In fact, it could very well be, for all we know."

She taps her chin with her index finger. "Maybe we should kiss. It might jog your memory."

Hope soars through my chest. Is Alex really suggesting that we kiss? I don't even care that it's to see if I can remember anything, I just want my mouth on hers.

"Great idea!" I exclaim. My cheeks heat, and I look away, too embarrassed by my over-enthusiasm.

"Are you nervous?" The question is quiet and tentative.

I force myself to look Alex in her eyes. If we are going to do something as intimate as kissing, then I need to be honest with her. "Yes."

She smiles at me. "Me too. Let's do this."

I gaze into her hazel eyes, my nerves dancing in my heart. My lack of memory is not doing me any favors right now. What if I'm not a good kisser? I want this to be a good experience for both Alex and me, even if she sees this as just a memory-jogging exercise.

But what if it's not? She did say she finds me attractive. But I can't overthink it. While I can stare into Alex's eyes forever, I need to make a move. I place a hand on her cheek and lean in, lightly grazing my lips against hers.

If Disney movies taught me anything, it's that kisses are a magical experience. There's a swell of romantic music, and you know the two characters have found true love. There's no music, but there's definitely magic. Something clicks. This kiss is my destiny.

I pull her closer, deepening the kiss. She gasps but relaxes into me. Her lips are softer than I imagined and fit perfectly against mine. My hands move to her hair, and I tangle my fingers in her silky tresses. I'm weightless, and she's my anchor.

The memories come flooding back. I've never kissed anyone before, and now I know why. I was saving my first kiss for my mate, my one true partner in life. That's why my tentacles reach for Alex. It's why her presence calms me. Everything makes sense now. Alex is my mate.

And as if my body can't process the magic of our kiss while also maintaining my disguise, I begin to transform, the fabric of my dress ripping in the process. I'm too lost in our kiss to care. I need more. My tentacles slither up her body, wrapping around her arms and waist, pulling her closer to me. A tentacle gently circles her neck, suctioning to the delicate skin of her throat. My heart swells when she moans against my mouth.

"What the fuck?" Avery screams, startling me from the most important moment of my life.

I thought she went to bed?

"What the fuck are you?" Avery's eyes are wide and full of fear.

Alex struggles in my grasp. "Fuck! Maris! You transformed!"

Even though it pains me, I drop my tentacles, allowing her to slip from my embrace.

"I couldn't help myself." I suck in a deep breath. "Alex, you're my mate."

Her face pales, and she backs away from me. "I'm your what? What the fuck does that mean?"

My heart sinks. I finally find my mate, and she rejects me.

Chapter 7
Alex

Maris looks like I just slapped her by asking for clarification on the 'mate' thing. What does that even mean? Is she using British slang for a friend? Or does she mean like wolves and birds and other breeding animals? I can't handle the idea of this having to do with breeding. How would that even work?

And what about that kiss? *Holy shit!* I've never experienced anything like it. All that mattered was her lips on mine and her tentacles pulling me tight against her. Everything else melted away, especially when one of her tentacles wrapped around my neck. The gentle suckling on my throat's sensitive skin sent tingles up my spine.

But I can't think about that right now. Especially with my sister screaming and cowering against the wall. What is she even doing out of the guest room?

"Please tell me what the hell is going on!"

"Avery, please try to calm down." I attempt to soothe with a calming voice. "I can only focus on one thing at a time." I need to process Maris's declaration before I can handle Avery.

Avery lets out a whimper of protest before clamping her hands over her mouth. Maybe she will be quiet long enough for me to wrench an answer from Maris. However, the kraken looks like she is about to burst into tears. I doubt I'll get any response if she devolves into a blubbering mess.

"Maris," I say, brows creased. "What do you mean by 'mate?'"

She cringes at me, regret etched on her face. It pains me. I want to go back in time and force myself to be kinder instead of freaking the fuck out. The compulsion to touch and comfort Maris is too strong. I place a hand on her shoulder.

"You can tell me," I urge.

She looks at my hand with longing before holding my gaze with those mesmerizing gold eyes.

"It means we are destined to be together," Maris whispers.

What did she just say? Who ordains something like this? Is this forever? But even as my mind races with millions of questions, my heart pounds.

Maris continues, her tentacles gently writhing, "I have waited my whole life for my mate. I should have known from the first moment I saw you, but it wasn't until I kissed you that the bond became clear. Alex, if you accept me as your mate, I will devote myself to you until my dying breath. With each push and pull of their waves, the tides will sing your name so that even the moon will know you. There is no devotion like a kraken to their mate."

Her words shatter me. Her dying breath? My last girlfriend broke up with me because I wasn't committed enough. I haven't dated since. Not because I am still hung up on her or anything, but because I just never cared enough about anyone to dedicate myself. My knees quake, leaving me suddenly unsteady on my feet. I can't breathe. Maris's confession is enormous and daunting.

Maris grabs my shoulders and wraps her tentacles around my legs, steadying me. For a brief moment, her touch soothes me. But then her words come rushing back, and I feel trapped in her embrace.

"Let me go," I beseech in a whisper.

"I apologize." She turns away, releasing her hold on me, but not before I see the hurt in her eyes.

I'm torn between comforting her and running away. She just laid her heart out to me, but I can't handle it. Being someone's mate is an entirely new concept to me. There's no denying the chemistry between Maris and me. The pull to her is strong. I've never felt anything like it. But exploring a relationship with Maris feels impossible. For one, she's a mythical sea monster. For another, I don't know if I can devote myself to her like a mate should.

"No need to apologize, Maris," I plead, hoping to throw a Band-Aid over the gaping wound I've given her. "I've never heard of mates before, at least not in this capacity, and it's a lot to process. I don't know if I am ready for that kind of commitment. Besides, how could a human and a kraken even be mates?"

Avery gasps. "A kraken? Like the old myth?"

Maris turns to her. "Yes. I am a kraken."

She narrows her eyes as she approaches me. "And you knew this, Alex?"

I nod. "When I rescued Maris, she looked like this."

"And you didn't think to tell me?" she asks, placing her hands on her hips.

I blink at her. What happened to my cowering sister? Now she's back to acting like she runs the show.

"Um...weren't you just freaking out a few seconds ago?"

"But now I know what's going on." Avery clears her throat. "You saved Maris when she was a kraken. For some reason, you decide to keep this a secret from your big sister. You and Maris are friends with sexual tension. You kiss. Maris realizes you two are fated life partners. You're now freaking out because you have commitment issues. Did I miss anything?"

Maris lets out a nervous chuckle. "I also lost all my memories, and we are working together to recover them."

Avery nods. "Makes sense."

My jaw drops. I always knew my sister was adaptable, but this situation is so bonkers. I can barely wrap my head around it, and I've had a little over 24 hours to process. How can she accept everything so easily?

I cross my arms over my chest. "That's bullshit."

"Is it?" Avery grins. "Or are you just pissed I hit the nail on the head?"

I glare at her. "I thought you went to bed."

She shrugs. "I was thirsty, so I came to get a glass of water."

"You weren't spying on us?" I ask, narrowing my eyes.

"Ew." Avery walks over to the cabinet, grabs a glass, and fills it from the fridge's water filter. "It may have been weird of me to suggest you kiss her as a dare, but spying on my little sister kissing? That's creepy as fuck."

While her answer is annoying, I believe her.

"Besides." She beams. "Aren't you glad we decided to have a slumber party?"

"I think you mean *you* decided to have a slumber party."

Avery grins. "Semantics. My point is that now I can help with memory recovery."

As the older sister, Avery has always been bossy. While her domineering personality grates my nerves sometimes, she always means well. Besides, it might be helpful for her to be here since things will likely be awkward between me and Maris. And having another mind working to solve Maris's memory problems doesn't hurt.

"You're right," I grumble. "It would be nice to have you around."

Avery turns to Maris. "I'm sorry. I didn't ask you. Are you okay with me helping out?"

Maris smiles. "Of course! I'm so grateful you want to help.

"What are friends for?" Avery drains her glass of water. "Now, I have a few questions about being a kraken and this whole mate thing, especially since it has to do with my little sister. So, buckle the fuck up."

I groan. "No! Avery, please go to bed. I've already agreed to let you stick around. Isn't that enough for tonight?"

"You expect me to just go to bed after this?"

"Yes," I answer, deadpan.

After staring at me for a few moments, Avery rolls her eyes. "Fine. But I better get some answers tomorrow." She points to Maris. "You may be my new best friend, but that doesn't mean you get a free pass. I need to know your intentions with Alex."

I throw my hands in the air. "Can you not do the whole 'overbearing big sister thing' right now?"

Avery sighs. "Whatever. Just don't do anything I wouldn't do."

Before I can open my mouth to retort, Avery is already halfway down the hall.

"Good night, lovebirds," she calls as the guest room door opens and closes, followed by the soft click of the lock.

Maris and I are officially alone.

"I'm sorry, Alex," Maris says barely above a whisper.

"Why?" I ask, rubbing my temples. This is exhausting.

"I shouldn't have sprung the fact that you are my mate on you. I'm sure it's overwhelming."

"Humans don't have mates." I nod. "Many of us get married, but honestly, even the concept of marriage intimidates me."

"Because you struggle with commitment?"

I sigh. "The idea of belonging to someone doesn't interest me. Maybe it's because I've never cared enough about anyone to feel that way. Or perhaps it's because I'm just not capable. I don't know, but I need time to process."

Maris chews her lip, her tentacles twitching in agitation. "You don't have to."

"What do you mean?"

"You don't have to be my mate." She stares at the floor. "You can choose not to accept it."

I perk up. "I can?"

"Yes. No one is forcing us to be mates."

Relief washes over me. I want to be the master of my fate. Control over my own life is essential to me. I may make boring choices, but they are still mine. Being with Maris should be up to me and her, not some invisible power or whatever writes our destiny.

But do I want to be with Maris? I keep thinking back to the magic of our kiss. If I am being honest with myself, the kiss felt like it was meant to be. I wish things were different. If only Maris weren't an immortal sea creature who belongs in the ocean. Why couldn't she be human? We could date and get to know each other slowly. And yet, it's not her human form that makes my heart flutter. She's attractive in both forms, but as a kraken, she is captivating.

"That's excellent news," I admit. "If we get together, I want it to be because we choose to."

A ghost of a smile tugs at the corners of Maris's mouth. "I understand. No one wants to feel like they don't have control over their own life."

I exhale, relaxing my tense muscles. "I'm thankful that you acknowledge why this is hard for me. My mind is also buzzing with a billion questions."

"Like what?"

"Where to start?" I sit back at the table and reach for a now-cold slice of pizza, desperate for something to occupy my hands. "How can you even be mates with a human?"

Maris doesn't join me, choosing to slither back and forth across the living room instead. "Humans and krakens aren't too different, if you think about it."

"What are you talking about?" I hold back a laugh. "You literally have tentacles!"

"Sure." She nods. "Physically, there are some differences. But do we not feel and think the same?"

I chew a bite of pizza slowly to give myself time to consider what Maris said. She's right. Emotionally and mentally, Maris and I process things the same. We both have unique personalities and motivations. It's only the physical aspects that set us apart.

"Have a kraken and a human ever had a successful relationship?"

Maris rubs her chin. "I'm not sure. What are you worried about?"

"How would it work? You belong in the ocean, and I belong on dry land."

Maris pauses and locks her eyes with mine, her mouth set in a determined line. "The fates wouldn't intertwine us if it couldn't work."

I fight the urge to agree with her. Logically, we shouldn't work, but when I consider the way our lips fit together so well, it makes sense. My cheeks heat. What would sex be like? Would she use her tentacles? I squeeze my thighs together, fighting the tingling sensation growing between my legs.

Maris's eyebrow quirks. "Are you okay?"

Oh shit. Does she know I'm getting aroused? How would she even be able to detect that?

I inhale a deep breath, preparing to lie through my teeth. "I'm fine. Just tired."

Maris's eyes narrow. I'm a terrible liar, and she knows this about me. It's such a little fib. Maybe she will let it slide. I don't have the mental or physical energy to explain that her tentacles make me horny.

"It is late. We can finish this discussion another time."

Thank god she let it go.

"I would like that." While I want answers to all my questions, this conversation has taken its toll on me. The dull ache of desire isn't helping the situation either. I need some sleep.

"I do not want you to feel rushed." Maris shakes her head. "Promise me you'll take time to process and decide."

I offer her an appreciative smile. Even when Maris is clearly in pain, she still cares about my comfort. Is this the devotion she was speaking of? Or is it just Maris's kindness shining through?

"Thank you." I rise from my seat. "I know you are itching for some water. Do you want to soak before bed?"

"You are incredible." Maris lets out a huge breath. "I would appreciate that."

She follows me to my bathroom. We are silent as I fill the giant tub. To my surprise, it's not awkward, even though it should be. It's comfortable and warm. Many things could be said, but we choose to bask in the comfort of each other's company.

When Maris slips into the water, careful not to make a mess, she closes her eyes and smiles. "This is what I needed."

"I bet it doesn't feel as good as the ocean." I skim my fingers across the water's surface. "I'm sorry we didn't get there tonight. My sister kind of threw a wrench in everything."

A tentacle gently wraps around my wrist. "It's okay. I adore your sister."

I stroke her velvety skin with my thumb. It's a mesmerizing sensation, one that I can't get enough of. Without thinking, I circle a sucker with my finger, lost in her touch.

Maris shivers, and I jerk my hand out of her grip. "I'm sorry!"

"No. You're fine." The skin on her cheeks darkens. "My suckers are very sensitive."

I bury my face in my hands. "Shit! Now I'm even more sorry!" Was stroking her sucker the equivalent of nibbling my ear?

"You couldn't have known." Maris clears her throat. "Anyway, I only need a few more minutes."

Thank fuck Maris changed the subject. While there's a part of me that thinks learning the sexual anatomy of a kraken sounds intriguing, I'm too tired to dive into that right now.

"No problem! I'll go make up the couch." I head for the door.

She cocks her head. "What do you mean?"

"I'll sleep in the living room."

"Why would you do that?"

"Uh...Avery is in the guest room, and you can't fit on the sofa as a kraken, so you'll need my bed."

"I've seen your bed." Maris gives me a quizzical look. "We could both easily fit."

"No!" I cough. "We are not sharing a bed. I need the space to think."

"Oh." Maris's face and tentacles droop. "I get it. It's for the best. I still don't know if I can keep my tentacles from touching you. That might be annoying when trying to sleep."

My imagination flashes to being wrapped up in her tentacles, my legs held open, and one inching its way up my thigh. *Fuck! Stop being horny for the kraken.*

"Right. Uh...annoying." I let out an anxious chuckle. "Just drain the tub when you finish soaking, and I'll see you in the morning."

"Okay." Maris bites her lip. "Good night, Alex."

"Good night, Maris."

Chapter 8
Maris

Sunlight seeps through the curtains. I didn't sleep. How could I? I've found my mate, and she doesn't know if she wants me. The worst part is that I know she feels the pull towards me. There's no way she can't. The mating bond is intense, and I felt the way she melted into my kiss. Why would she deny that? Is my devotion repulsive?

I'm not going to sleep now, and I can't lie in Alex's bed any longer. I should be comforted, as the pillows and linens smell like her, but I'm starving for her. I had a taste, and now I don't know if I'll ever be satisfied.

As I make my way to the door, I listen for the movements of Avery or Alex. I freeze when soft footsteps approach the room. One of the sisters is awake. Did sleep help Alex make her decision? Has she come to seal my fate?

A quiet knock compels me forward. I inhale deeply, steeling myself for the worst yet hoping for the best. When I open the door to see Avery, a rush of conflicting emotions overtakes me. Relief and disappointment course through me but my overriding emotion is confusion. Why is Avery here?

She eyes me from head to tentacle tip. "I forgot just how striking you are. Can I come in?"

I open the door wider to allow her entry. "Striking?"

"Yeah." Avery flops onto the bed. "You are magnificent, especially as a kraken."

My eyes widen. Avery is so nonchalant compared to her sister. Even Thomas was more formal when he complimented my appearance.

She chuckles. "I wasn't coming onto you, by the way. Abundant compliments are a benefit of our friendship."

I grin, pleased that Avery still considers us friends. "Thank you."

Her grin falters. "But before we go too far down the friendship path, I need to know something."

"Anything."

"Is she really your mate?" Avery asks with a frown. "I mean, what does that even mean? Is this some weird way to get her to have sex with you? Wait. Can you two even have sex?"

"I would never have sexual relations with Alex without her consent." I cringe, disgusted she would even suggest such a thing.

Avery holds up her hands in surrender. "Alright. I believe you. But I still want to know more about what it means to be mates."

I get where Avery is coming from. Humans don't have 'mates.' Of course this would be confusing for her. Plus, I appreciate her being concerned for Alex. Anyone who cares this much for my mate's wellbeing has earned my respect.

"It means fate has drawn us together. Krakens only get one mate in their lifetime. And to me, it means cherishing and taking care of her until the day I die or the world ends, whichever comes first. I'm so blessed to have someone like Alex as my mate."

"But you're basically a walking ray of sunshine, and Alex is...not. In fact, she can be downright unpleasant at times. Are you sure you're willing to deal with that until the end of time?"

I tilt my head. "Do you really think that about her?"

Avery smirks. "No. And I take you don't think that way about her either."

"Nope," I respond with a smile. "Underneath that rough exterior is someone kind and considerate. I don't know why she puts up such a front, but I hope to one day find out."

Avery's gaze is unwavering and scrutinizing, but eventually a smile crinkles the corners of her eyes.

"Alex is an idiot," she declares.

"What do you mean?" I have no idea where Avery is going with this.

She sighs impatiently as if I should know exactly what she is saying. "Oh, come on, Maris. I see Alex on the couch, and you're in here alone. I can only assume she didn't fall into your arms and accept that she is your mate, even though you clearly care a lot about her."

I can't handle Avery's knowing stare. She pegged the situation perfectly, and I hate it. If only I could tell her the night ended with Alex accepting the bond. Instead, I'm alone, dejected, and frightened.

"Hey." Avery pats the bed, indicating I should sit next to her. "Alex may be an idiot right now, but she'll come around."

I join her on the bed. "You think?"

"I witnessed that kiss. It was more magical than a Disney kiss!"

"Was it like a Princess kiss?" I sit up.

She nods. "I wouldn't have been surprised if fireworks went off. And even through my freak out over your transformation, I could feel the chemistry between you two."

"It was the most perfect moment of my life." I bury my face in my hands. "I just wish she had felt the same way about it."

Avery pats my back. "I am positive she felt it, too. Just give her time. She's slow to process her feelings."

I stiffen. How much time does Alex need? What is considered slow to the sisters? I don't have much time.

"Wait." Avery frowns. "There's something you're not telling me."

I search her eyes. Can I trust her with the truth? I don't know if I can handle admitting it aloud. That will make it real. If I keep my secret, I can pretend this nightmare isn't happening.

Avery takes my hands in hers. "You can tell me."

"You can't tell Alex."

Avery doesn't soothe my soul like Alex, but her friendship comforts me like Thomas's. Unburdening my sorrows with him always helped. Maybe the same will be true with Avery.

She chews the inside of her cheek, and a contemplative hum escapes her pursed lips. "I hate keeping secrets from my sister."

"Then I won't burden you, because Alex cannot know."

"We're friends." She squeezes my hands. "I will keep your secret. I just want to let you know how I feel about it."

"I appreciate your honesty." I suck in a deep breath. It's

now or never. "If Alex doesn't accept the mating bond, I will die."

Avery's jaw drops. I instantly regret telling her. This knowledge is not something she should have to bear.

"I—" she stammers. "I just... Are you serious?"

"Yes. It's one of the only ways a kraken can perish."

Avery rises from the bed. "You can't not tell Alex this!" Her voice is too loud and shrill. It will surely wake Alex.

"Shhh! She can't know."

She lowers her voice. "Why not?"

"Because I don't want to pressure her to accept the bond," I whisper. "The ability to make her own choices is important to her."

"Sure!" Avery begins pacing the room. "But Alex would never forgive herself if you died because of her."

"She would never know."

She freezes, her eyes narrowing at me. "What do you mean by that?"

I stayed up all night thinking about this and came up with the perfect solution. "If Alex rejects the mating bond, I will return to the ocean to die in peace," I declare, lifting my chin.

"No!" Avery shakes her head. "I don't accept that answer. You can't do that."

"What else do you propose?" Tears blur my vision, over-whelmed by the helplessness of the situation. "The guilt would eat Alex alive. Besides, I want her to be with me because she wants to, not because she feels obligated to save my life."

She throws her hands in the air. "This is ridiculous!"

"But there isn't another solution."

Avery collapses onto the bed with a frustrated groan. "I know we just met, but you're still my friend. I don't want anything to happen to you. Alex would also miss you. Even if she stupidly spurns you, she will regret it one day. I know she will."

Avery's passion for her sister is moving. I understand. Alex is special and deserves nothing but happiness.

I wipe at the tear that trickles down my cheek. "It's better she lives in blissful ignorance than feeling trapped."

Avery sighs. "How much time does she have to make the decision?"

"Once I feel the pull of the mating bond, we have until the next full moon to seal it."

She whips out her phone. "Siri, when is the next full moon?" Avery's eyes widen when the results populate on her screen. "Maris, the next full moon is four days from now."

I draw in a long breath. "I know." As a creature born from the tides, I know the moon intimately—my magic is tied to her. I feel her push and pull the tides, and even while I'm out of the comfort of the ocean, I sense her.

"That's not much time! You could be dying by next week."

"I have been awake all night coming to terms with it," I admit. "I believe what you put into the universe is what you get back. That's why I always try to be positive, even in the face of adversity. I didn't let myself despair when I woke up with no memories. I knew that if I kept high spirits, I was more likely to get my memories back. But this? I don't know, Avery. This is relying on another person's free will."

Avery wraps her arms around me. "It will be okay. Alex will make the right decision. Try to keep that sunshiny disposition you have. It's special, and I know she sees that, too."

I allow myself the comfort of Avery's embrace. She

reminds me of Thomas. Honest and kind, maybe a little sassier than Thomas, but with a heart of gold, just like him. I miss my friend, but I'm thankful to have a new one who can be here for me during such a difficult time.

After a few moments, I reluctantly pull away. "Thank you, Avery. In the end, Alex's happiness is all that matters. She needs to make the best decision for her."

She frowns. "But what about you?"

"That's the thing about a kraken's commitment. We devote everything to our mates; if they reject us, our lives don't have meaning."

Avery cringes. "That's kind of morbid."

I chuckle. "Most krakens go their entire lifetime without finding their mate. I'm extremely blessed to have found one in Alex, even if she doesn't accept me."

"What's that old saying?" Avery pushes her hair back from her face. "Better to have loved and lost than never loved at all or some shit?"

"I've never heard that sentiment, but it makes sense." I twist my lips into a wry smile.

Avery stands and motions for me to follow her into the bathroom. "Let's clean the tears from your face so Alex doesn't get suspicious."

"You'll keep my secret?"

She lays her hand on her chest. "I promise."

I smile gratefully. "Thank you."

After I rinse off and Avery deems me presentable, we make our way into the kitchen. I try not to look at Alex on the couch as we pass the living room, but her gentle snoring fills my ears.

Avery rummages through the cabinets, making a ruckus.

"Hey!" I whisper. "You'll wake Alex."

Avery shrugs. "That bitch can sleep all day. It's best to wake her up with the sounds and smells of breakfast."

"I tried that the other day, and she wasn't too pleased. She just ate a banana."

"Of course." Avery rolls her eyes. "Bananas are her favorite. I'll chop one up to make her peanut butter and banana toast. That will make her happy. What do you want?"

"I like eggs," I answer, my mouth watering.

"How do you like them cooked?"

"Raw."

Avery blinks at me. "You know. I just found out krakens are real, but you eating raw eggs is the most bizarre thing I've heard in the past 24 hours."

A groan from the couch diverts our attention. "Maris has peculiar food tastes." Alex sits up, revealing the most spectacular bedhead.

"I've noticed." Avery takes a carton of eggs out of the icebox. "Maris, I'm not serving you raw eggs. It's time you try a hot breakfast. I bet you would love sunny-side-up eggs."

I quirk an eyebrow. "Sunny-side-up?"

"Yes. The yolk will still be runny."

Alex yawns and pads into the kitchen. "Will you scramble mine?"

Avery rolls her eyes. "Sure. But only because you're my favorite sister."

"I'm your only sister." Alex crosses her arms over her chest.

"Whatever. Go do something about your hair," Avery says, waving a spatula at Alex's hair.

Alex brings her hands to her hair. A small squeak emits

when she tries to run her fingers through her tangled tresses.

"Excuse me." She rushes down the hall towards her bedroom.

I fight the urge to follow her and offer help. My fingers would have no problem combing through the snarls. But I know I can't. Alex needs her space. I can't smother her with my affection.

Avery giggles. "She likes you."

My heart skips a hopeful beat. "You think?"

"If it were anyone else, she would have told me to take a hike. She got worried about her appearance because you're here."

My face heats. "That's cute."

"Honestly, watching my sister get so flustered is quite adorable." Avery cracks several eggs into the sizzling pan. "I haven't seen her get so worked up since her first crush in the sixth grade."

Jealousy flashes through me, hot and sour. I shouldn't envy Alex's previous romantic interests, but the mating bond tends to cloud judgment. My tentacles coil in on themselves.

"Did you just get jealous?" Avery chuckles.

"I can't help it." I focus on the bunch of bananas on the counter, hoping to calm the sting of resentment. Maybe if I stare at the disgusting fruit long enough, I can forget about Alex having crushes on people who aren't me.

"Is this part of the mating bond?" Avery asks, grabbing various dishes from the cabinets.

"It can make logical decision-making a bit fuzzy regarding my mate."

"No need to be jealous. Trust me. Alex's exes were so boring compared to you."

I grin, grateful for her ability to soothe the jealousy writhing beneath my skin. "That feels like high praise."

Alex's bedroom door closes with a soft thud. "What is high praise?" she asks, running her fingers through her now-tamed hair.

Avery places two eggs on a plate and slides the dish towards me. "I was just telling Maris that she's pretty amazing."

Longing flickers in Alex's eyes. Her gaze fixates on me, and she smiles softly. "She is, isn't she?"

My tentacles squirm, reaching for her, encouraged by the yearning on her face. I could easily change that look to one of pleasure. It would be so simple. I just need to slide a tentacle down the front of those thick pajama pants and find the delectable scent that calls to me from between her legs.

One of my tentacles grazes Alex's leg. She lets out a soft gasp, jerking away from me. I inhale sharply, startled by her sudden act of revulsion. Weren't we having a moment?

"Sorry," Alex stammers. "You should taste your eggs."

My mouth forms into a tight-lipped grin. If she wants to move on without acknowledging what just passed between us, I'll let her. "No worries. I need to get them under control." I look at my plate of breakfast to shift my focus off Alex.

Avery places a fork next to my plate. "You won't insult me if you don't like them."

The eggs smell delicious. Their aroma isn't as appetizing as the pizza, but my mouth waters all the same. I cut into the egg with my fork and shovel the goopy mess into my mouth. The yolk is fatty, smooth, and enhanced by the perfect amount of pepper and salt.

"Avery," I moan. "This is incredible."

She raises her eyebrows and smiles. "Yeah? Better than raw eggs?"

"Absolutely." I bypass the stupid fork and tilt the plate back, allowing the eggs to slide directly into my mouth.

"Uhh…" Avery's mouth hangs open as she watches me chew. "I forgot about your, um, enthusiasm for food."

Alex waves a hand through the air, dismissing Avery's growing horror. "You should see her eat a seafood boil."

Avery chuckles. "I'm not sure I want to see that."

I swallow just in time to let out a boisterous laugh without spewing eggs everywhere. "I'll let your rude comment slide if you make me more eggs."

Avery rolls her eyes. "I'm hungry too, you know." She looks at Alex. "Teach your girlfriend to make her own eggs."

Alex sets her mouth in a firm line. "Maris is not my girlfriend."

"Oh. That's right. She's your mate."

"Avery!" Alex blushes. "Will you shut up?"

I also want Avery not to tease Alex. Usually, I would love to watch Alex's face turn adorable shades of pink. But not right now. I understand that Avery is trying to force Alex to think about our predicament, but I don't know if embarrassing her about it is the best idea.

"Only if you teach Maris to make eggs." Avery passes the spatula to Alex. "I have to start on your toast."

Alex's glower morphs into open adoration. "Are you making me banana toast?"

Avery nods.

"With extra cinnamon?"

"Of course." Avery scoffs playfully. "What kind of big sister would I be if I didn't give you extra cinnamon?"

Alex grabs me by my hand, yanking me towards the stove. "Alright, Maris. Time to learn to cook an egg."

I do my best to pay attention to what she says, but being close to Alex when she's this excited distracts me. She's so beautiful. I have to force my tentacles to remain still.

Despite Alex's endless patience, I manage to burn two attempts at eggs. Alex lets out an impatient sigh, but the corner of her mouth quirks, letting me know she's not actually frustrated with me.

"Allow me," she says gently, taking the pan from me.

She hums to herself as she prepares the rest of my breakfast. My heart expands as I watch her. There's something special about my mate cooking food for me. I can't wait to develop my skills so I can one day make her a meal to show how much this means to me.

When Alex places the eggs onto the plate, she does so with a proud smile.

"Thank you." I reach for the food, but she bats my hand away.

"I haven't seasoned them yet." Alex reaches for not only the salt and pepper but also a bottle of red liquid. "You have to try these with hot sauce."

She passes me the food after adding a few splashes. "Here."

I sniff at the eggs. A peppery sensation tickles my nose, making my eyes water. "Oh, my goddess! Is this made with chilis like the seafood boil?

Alex nods. "If you liked the shrimp from the other night, you'll like hot sauce."

I offer a large grin before tilting the eggs into my mouth. It's spicier than the seafood boil, but I like how it makes my mouth tingle.

"These are even better than Avery's," I exclaim once I finish my eggs.

Alex giggles. "I knew you would like them with a bit of heat."

I can't help myself. A tentacle snakes up Alex's body and strokes her cheek. "You know me so well."

She closes her eyes and leans into my touch. The sounds of Avery preparing Alex's toast fade away. All I can see is Alex's blissful expression. All I can hear is her dreamy sigh. All I can feel is her soft skin. All that matters is Alex and her acceptance of this moment.

"Thank you for making the tastiest thing I've ever eaten," I whisper into her ear.

Alex blinks, her cheeks flushing pink before she backs away. "You don't know that. You can't remember anything before two days ago."

I shudder at the loss of her skin against mine. "I do know. Surely I would remember eating something so delicious."

Alex averts her eyes, but I don't miss the slight smirk on her lips. I can't help the triumph that swells in my chest. *This is progress, right?*

She focuses on what Avery is doing. "Is that my toast?" Alex wiggles past me to grab a plate filled with scrambled eggs and two slices of bread piled high with a spread and chopped bananas.

I point to the brown substance. "What's that?"

Avery's jaw drops. "It's peanut butter! Have you never had peanut butter?" She dips a spoon into a jar of the stuff, scooping a large dollop, before offering it to me. "Try it."

I tentatively lick at the paste. And immediately gag. It's earthy but way too sweet. "What the fuck did you just feed me?"

Alex takes a giant chomp of her toast. I nearly retch again, watching her. Bananas and peanut butter? My mate may be perfect, but her palette is horrendous.

"I'm starting to think you hate sweet things," she suggests around a bite of food.

I chew the tip of a claw as I attempt to remember. "You know, I think you're right. Thomas once fed me an orange, and I hated it."

Avery laughs. "The mystery I want to solve about you is how you know about things like cribbage but not pizza or peanut butter. How is that even possible?"

Alex swallows her bite of toast. "I've been thinking about that, as well. Maris, you pretty much remember things as you experience them?"

I nod slowly, wondering where she's going with this line of thinking.

"I am starting to think you stopped experiencing human culture at some point. Obviously, you have been exposed because of Thomas, but I wonder when he lived." She pulls out her phone and taps around for a moment. "Poker was invented in the early 1800s, so you must have ended your involvement with humans before then."

A contemplative hum emits from Avery. "You know, I think you're onto something." She claps her hands together. "I have an idea!"

"What is it?" Alex and I ask in unison.

"What if we watched historical nautical documentaries?" She looks at me. "We can figure out what you remember and what you don't. Was Thomas a pirate?"

"He was."

"Excellent." Avery points at Alex. "Clean up while I search for documentaries."

"Why me?" Alex whines.

"Because I made breakfast," Avery quips.

"I also cooked."

Avery frowns. "Are you going to make Maris clean, then?"

"No." Alex clenches her jaw.

"That's what I thought." Avery prances to the living room. "Maris, come sit next to me."

"Alright." Avery clears her throat as we wrap up our last documentary. "We can determine that Maris stopped interacting with humans sometime in the early 1800s, right before piracy was eliminated in the Western part of the world."

The living room is bathed in an orange glow from the sunset. We've been watching pirate documentaries all day, only pausing for restroom and snack breaks. I remembered some people, places, and events, but there were also large chunks of information that I didn't recall.

Alex chews on her thumbnail, her eyebrows furrowed in concentration. "I agree. I think our next step should be getting you in the ocean like we intended last night."

Avery looks at her phone. "The sun should be set within the next 15 minutes. But as much as I would love to go with you, I have to get home. I have a meeting tomorrow with a major new client. Apparently, my demo reel showcasing my 3D animations is getting passed around."

Alex stiffens. "It shouldn't take us that long."

"You'll be fine." Avery places a hand on her shoulder.

I understand why Alex doesn't want to be alone with me, but it still hurts. However, I can't show it. I plaster a neutral look on my face and keep quiet, allowing the sisters to talk.

Avery makes her way to the front door. "I hope to see you again soon, Maris." She points to Alex, eyes narrowing. "You better report back tonight. If you don't, I will hunt you down."

"Yeah, yeah." Alex scoffs. "I know the drill. I don't want you showing up unannounced again."

With a final wave, Avery exits the house, leaving me and Alex alone.

I clear my throat. "Should we get going?" I don't want to dwell here and make things more awkward than they need to be.

She nods, a small smile on her lips. "The beach is a short ride away."

"Give me a second." I rush to the guest room and transform into my human shape. It already feels unnatural, but it's what I must do if I want to return to my home.

Before I leave the room, I slip on one of the cute dresses Alex bought me yesterday. I twirl before the full-length mirror in the corner. At least I get to wear a gift from my mate.

My heart hammers the entire drive. What if nothing happens? If I don't recover my memories, what will we do next? Thankfully, as Alex promised, reaching our destination doesn't take long, which is perfect because it doesn't give my anxieties about being back in the ocean time to fester.

It's beautiful in the faint moonlight. We finally park in

an empty lot. Tears form in my eyes when Alex kills the moped engine. I can hear the crash of the waves against the sand. I am almost home.

"I figure you can jump in from there," Alex says, pointing to a pier near where we parked.

I nod, bouncing from one foot to another in anticipation of being in the ocean. I follow Alex, the smell of brine comforting. She looks at me with lifted brows when we reach the edge of the pier.

The water below is dark and daunting. I ache to be back in, but I'm anxious. What if the ocean doesn't welcome me home? I look at Alex. Her facial expression is one I've not seen before, almost as if she bit into something too sweet.

"Are you okay?" I inquire, turning to face her.

She shivers when a cool breeze ruffles her hair. "Don't worry about me. This moment is about you."

What is going through Alex's mind? This may be my moment, but I can't imagine being here without her.

I hold out my hand. "Come with me?"

Alex's eyebrows knit together. Her eyes dart between my hand and my gaze. "Why?"

"I can't do this without you."

She bites her lip and continues to stare at my hand. My heart drops. I will have to do this on my own, without my mate and her support.

Just as I am about to give up and go alone, she gives me a soft smile and takes my hand. "Let's do this."

Alex averts her eyes when I shed my dress, and remains fully clothed. Is she just going to jump in like that? But I don't press her. Despite being uncomfortable with my nudity, she still takes my hand as we step to the pier's edge together.

There's no need to count down. Somehow, we know when to jump in. We both inhale and take the plunge. With a splash, we submerge below the warm water. I'm home. And I have my mate with me.

Chapter 9
Alex

The water is warmer than I thought it would be. I didn't bring a swimsuit, so my clothes are soaked. But it doesn't matter. Nothing matters except being here for Maris.

What if she doesn't remember anything after being in the ocean? What if she does? I hate myself for it, but I'm afraid that by recovering her memories, she'll forget all about me. I may be her mate, but she said it was our choice. She could choose to leave me behind.

But Maris never lets go of my hand. Instead, she wraps a tentacle around my waist and pulls me to the surface faster than I can swim. She laughs when our heads break above the water. The delight on her face makes me smile. I love seeing her back in her real skin. Her human shape is beautiful, but nothing compares to her natural state.

"I'm in the ocean!" she squeals in delight.

"Do you remember anything?"

She shakes her head, but she doesn't look disappointed. "Not yet. I'm just so happy to be here. With you."

Maris doesn't remove her tentacle from around my

waist. I don't mind. Being in her embrace is precisely where I want to be. I've always felt a pull towards her, but since we kissed, my skin burns for her, and her touch is the only salve. I'm doing my best not to give in to my desire. I need some semblance of control. But I can't bring myself to squirm out of her grip. I feel safe in this big, dark ocean with her holding me.

She pulls me towards her, her smile bright in the moonlight. Maris's face is inches from mine. Her breath is against my lips. My heart races in my chest. The sounds of the ocean melt away. She's going to kiss me. And I'm not going to stop her.

Instead, her tentacles unwind from my body. "May I dive below the surface?"

I hold back a whine at the loss of her touch. I force a smile. "Of course. I'll be waiting here."

"I won't let anything happen to you." Maris tucks a wet lock of hair behind my ear.

I trust her completely, but I appreciate the reassurance. I nod, letting her know I'm grateful.

With a quiet splash, Maris slips beneath the surface. I keep my head above the gentle waves with ease. Part of lifeguard training is treading water with a brick over your head. I could do this for a while without tiring. But I decide to enjoy the quiet and float on my back. Usually, the beach would be noisy with the chattering and laughter of tourists and locals alike. But after dark, all that can be heard is the water's lapping against the sand the pier's wood.

"Shit!" Maris breaks the surface near to me. She hisses through her teeth, clutching a tentacle in her hand.

"What's wrong?" I swim towards her. The pale moon casts a soft light on her skin, revealing a dark liquid seeping from her. She's bleeding.

"I cut myself on something beneath the pier. You have to get out of the water. Now!"

Maris circles her tentacle around me and starts dragging me towards the pier. *Oh shit! Why is she freaking out?* My mind races with all the horror movies my sister has made me watch. Is she afraid of sharks? Or something worse? A few days ago, I didn't think krakens were real. What other horrors could be hiding in the depths of the ocean?

A chilling series of clicks and whistles sends a shiver up my spine. Maris climbs up the side of the pier. I've never been more thankful for her tentacles and suckers. I'm afraid to look behind us. What unearthly thing could have made that noise?

When she's about halfway up the side of the pier, Maris lifts me above her head, stretching her tentacle. "Grab onto the ledge."

"What about you?"

Maris shakes her head. "It's not me I'm worried about."

I desperately grasp the edge of the pier. My heart pounds. What could Maris be so afraid of? I scramble to lift myself and collapse with an exhausted cry on the rough wooden surface. But the danger isn't over. I need to check on Maris.

I creep towards the edge and peer over. Maris is still halfway up the wooden support beams, and right beneath her is the most terrifying creature I've ever seen. The moonlight reveals sickly gray skin covered in barnacles. Limp, thinning hair swirls in the water around it. Large, pupilless eyes like that of a deep-water fish peer up at me above a giant, grinning mouth of razor-sharp teeth.

What the fuck is that?

The creature gives a series of sharp whistles before

splashing its gnarled fishtail. It reaches for me with sinewy arms that end in jagged talons. I back away from the edge, terrified. Can that thing come out of the water after me? I want to get the fuck out of here, but I can't leave Maris behind.

"Maris!" I cry. "Hurry!"

But she ignores me, instead jumping back into the water and wrapping her tentacles around the monstrosity. Maris holds it out of the water by its neck. It squirms in her grasp, unable to do anything because her tentacles restrain its limbs.

I scream when it gnashes its teeth at Maris, but she lets out a smug laugh.

"You better settle down. If not, I'll allow you to slowly suffocate above the water instead of quickly ripping your hideous head from that pathetic body."

Desperate, choked clicks gurgle from the creature's mouth.

"What is that thing?" I squeak from above.

Maris gives it a rough shake. "It's a mermaid."

My jaw drops, stunned. That horror is a mermaid? Where did the legends that mermaids have sexy top halves come from? This thing looks like something straight out of Guillermo Del Toro's nightmares.

"You tried to attack my mate." Maris brings the mermaid within a few inches of her face.

I suck in a breath. She's too close. It could easily take a chunk out of her face.

"For that, I should end your life."

The mermaid emits more of those awful sounds that must be its speech.

"Speak in the human tongue of English so my mate can understand," Maris demands.

Its eyes dart to me. A long, putrid purple tongue slinks from behind its teeth and slides over its cracked white lips.

Maris tightens her squeeze on the mermaid's throat. "Don't even look at her."

It refocuses its attention on Maris. "But she looks so delicious." Its voice sounds like high-pitched, painful gargling from the back of its throat. I've never heard anything so chilling.

Before I can register what she's doing, Maris cocks her hand into a fist and lands a brutal jab against the mermaid's flat nose. It squeals, forcing me to cover my ears.

"That's your final warning," Maris snaps.

I would have never guessed that Maris has this kind of brutality in her. But it's not unwarranted. That creature would not hesitate to rip me to shreds. I always felt safe with Maris, but watching her protect me spreads heat throughout my body. I can't be getting turned on right now. There's a flesh-eating monster too close for my comfort.

"What do you want from me?" it croaks.

Maris tilts her head in my direction but keeps her sight trained on the mermaid. "What do you think, Alex? Does it deserve to live?"

Bile rises in my throat. She wants me to choose if this mermaid lives or dies. I can't make that heavy of a decision. I get that it tried to attack me, but Maris saved me, and now I'm safely out of the water. It can't hurt me anymore. Is murder necessary? She should show mercy and let it go.

But wait.

It could be of some use to us. Did it show up because of Maris's blood?

"Do you know why the mermaid showed up?" I ask, confident that I'm onto something.

"Kraken blood attracts particular creatures." Maris

explains, never taking her eyes off the mermaid. "Our blood has specific magical properties. It was bound to draw out anything nearby."

It's just as I thought. "Mermaid," I call, getting its attention. "Do you know of Maris?"

A hissing sound emits from its terrifying mouth that I soon recognize as a laugh. "Of course I do. Everyone knows of the Disappearing Maris."

I can't help the smug smile on my lips, even if I don't enjoy the term 'disappearing.' This mermaid knows about Maris. It may explain why she hasn't interacted with humans in 200 years.

Maris tilts her head. "I disappeared?"

The mermaid laughs again. "You must take me for a fool. I will reveal nothing." It nods towards me. "Not unless you give me her. I've never tasted the flesh of a kraken's mate. I wonder if it's sweeter than the last human I ate."

My blood chills. Maybe bargaining with a living nightmare isn't such a good idea.

"Never," Maris growls. "Try again."

"Fine." It closes its eyes as if thinking. After several of those creepy clicks, the mermaid looks at Maris again. "A taste of her blood."

Maris hums. "How about you tell us, or I kill you?"

This is going sour quickly. Something primal and protective has been triggered in Maris. If this mermaid keeps cajoling her, she's going to kill it. It obviously wants a taste of me, but there's no way Maris will agree to anything that harms me, and I'm not keen on the idea either. What could we give the mermaid that will satisfy it?

I snap my fingers as an idea strikes me. "Hair!"

Both Maris and the mermaid face me, waiting for me to continue.

"Would a lock of my hair suffice?" I lean forward, excited, and almost lose my footing. Thank fuck I collected myself before I fell in the water.

A large, toothy grin spreads over the mermaid's face.

"No!" Maris answers. "It can't have anything from you."

"Maris." I wish I could touch her and let her know it will be okay. "We can't let this opportunity slip away."

She stares at me for several moments as if waiting for me to change my mind. When I don't, she jostles the mermaid. "Will you accept a lock of my mate's hair?"

It licks its lips. "I accept."

I let out a sigh of relief, thankful we came to an agreement. I fish around in my pocket and pull out my utility knife. Flicking it open, I bring the sharp tool to my hair. This better be worth it. I slice off a chunk of my tresses right below my chin.

"Here." I hold the hair over the water.

Maris positions the mermaid under my hand so I can easily drop the hair into its open maw. It swallows my hair in one loud gulp before letting out a small belch. Maris's face twists in disgust, but she puts no more pressure on the mermaid's neck. I count that as a win.

"Alright, mermaid." I clear my throat. "What do you know of Maris?"

"Maris, the Great Protector, was the bane of our existence." It snarls at Maris. "You were always rescuing tasty morsels from shipwrecks. Most krakens cause them, but not you. It got worse when you befriended some famous sea captain. Even going so far as to interfere with mermaids, selkies, and kelpies."

Pride swells in my chest. Maris isn't a destructive beast

but rather a beacon of hope and safety in the dangerous sea. I wonder how many stories were told of her kindness.

The mermaid continues, "And when that captain died? It was spectacular. You destroyed his ship in your grief before disappearing beneath the waves. His crew were left to float at sea in their lifeboats for days. No one dared approach them, fearing your wrath. We waited for our opportunity, but the Royal Navy rescued them. And as far as we know, you never resurfaced."

Maris grimaces. After watching all the pirate documentaries, that likely means they were imprisoned or, worse, executed. I can't imagine what she's feeling right now. She loved Thomas's crew, and she essentially left them to die.

"Is that it?" I ask. That can't be it. There needs to be more.

"Yes," it hisses. "We all would have thought you were dead, but Caspian never went into mourning, so we all assumed you were still alive and he knew where you were. Trust me, he would have drained the seven seas if he couldn't find you."

"Caspian?" I question.

Maris's eyes go wide. "My father?"

I gasp. Of course, Maris has a father. She must have remembered him upon hearing his name.

The mermaid snickers. "The most feared creature in the ocean. But we all know he has a soft spot for his precious daughter."

"Where can we find Caspian?" I ask.

"Last I heard, he's in what you humans call the Bermuda Triangle."

The Bermuda Triangle freaks me out. Again, too many horror movies. But ideas are churning in my head. We have to get out there and find Maris's father. He is the next big lead in recovering her memories.

"Maris," I say her name softly.

Her eyes are wide and her mouth agape. She must be in shock. I need her to come back down to earth.

"Do you have any more questions for the mermaid?"

She lowers the mermaid but doesn't release her grip. "No."

"Then it's time to let it go."

"I'm going to release you," Maris snarls to the creature. "Are you aware of what I'm capable of?"

The mermaid nods.

"Are you going to try anything?"

It shakes its head.

"When I remove my tentacle from around your neck, you will turn around and swim away. If I catch you around this island again, I will tear you apart. Do you understand?"

"Yes, oh powerful one," it croaks.

"Never forget that Caspian is my father. I am just as capable of his brutality."

Maris unravels her tentacles from the mermaid. It rubs its neck, sore from where it was held. Keeping its gaze trained on her, it slowly backs away from Maris. Once it's outside of lunging distance from her, it turns around and dives below the water.

I hold my breath, waiting to see if the mermaid resurfaces, intending to hurt Maris. But after a few minutes, with no sign of it, Maris climbs out of the water and up the pier.

"Do you mind if I dry off before transforming again?" she explains before plopping down on the wooden planks. "I already ruined one dress you bought me."

"Of course." I lie down next to her, also needing to dry my soaked clothes a little more. "How are you feeling?"

"Angry." Her response is bitter.

"Why?"

"That thing could have hurt you," she admits with a flinch. "I was careless, allowing myself to bleed."

I scoff. "Nothing happened to me. I'm fine. You protected me."

Maris turns her face towards me. "You don't understand, Alex. As my mate, you are everything to me. If anything happened to you, it would destroy me."

My heart picks up speed. I can't help the excitement that rolls through me whenever she calls me her mate. The effect Maris has on me is pathetic. But I can't think about my feelings for her right now. We just uncovered significant facts about her. It's time to focus on that.

I clear my throat, pushing my thoughts to the side. "What do you think about what we discovered?"

She sighs. "I now remember glimpses of my father. He was always good to me, but he was brutal. I understand why he is the most feared monster in the ocean."

"I'm thinking we should find him."

Maris props up on her elbow. "I was thinking that too."

"Would your blood attract him?"

"Probably." She twirls a strand of wet hair between her fingers. "We would need to get to the Bermuda Triangle waters first."

I close my eyes, conjuring a map of the Atlantic Ocean and the surrounding landfall in my head. "If I recall correctly, the triangle starts right outside Miami. That's not too far. We can double-check when we get home."

She places a hand on top of mine. "Thank you, Alex. You have helped me far beyond what you originally agreed to."

I interlace my fingers with hers. "You still haven't recovered your memories of how you got into my pool. Besides, we're friends. I'll be here for you until you don't need me anymore."

Maris squeezes my hand. "I'll always need you."

Her words heat my cheeks. I should be fighting against this feeling. The most important thing is my choice, right? But would it really be so bad to give into the mating bond? I would have someone like Maris by my side for the rest of my years. But my life is so short compared to hers. Would she want to be tied to a mortal human? How long before she grows bored of me and feels trapped by our bond? I can't have that. I can't do that to either of us.

I sit up. "Are you dry enough to go home?"

Maris rises, transforming into a human as she does. She snags her discarded dress and pulls it over her head. "Let's go." She sounds dejected.

It hurts, knowing that I'm the one doing this to her. But she has to know it's for the best.

When we walk through the front door of my house, I quickly scoop up my phone and text Avery a high-level overview of what happened with a promise to call her tomorrow. She replies immediately with a thumbs-up emoji. I'm thankful she doesn't want to talk now. I'm exhausted and in desperate need of changing out of these wet clothes and a shower.

Maris transforms into a kraken, and I leave her on the sofa with a bag of carrots while I shower. As I bathe, I oscillate between planning our next steps for finding Caspian and how Maris's touch feels.

We could always rent a boat and sail a little past Miami. But also, did we almost kiss at the pier?

Maybe Caspian can tell us what happened to Maris. Would she have wrapped her tentacle around my neck again?

Back and forth until finally, the memory of kissing Maris wins. I want that again. A warmth spreads between my thighs as I imagine her lips on mine, her hands roaming my body, and her tentacles wrapped firmly around me.

My hand travels down my stomach. Just thinking about Maris kissing me makes me wet. I can't let my mind wander much further. That would be disastrous. Adding 'horny' to my list of problems isn't ideal. I crank the faucet as cold as possible without turning off the water. It should shock the arousal from my system. It works, kind of.

I hurry out of the shower, dry off quickly, and throw on my favorite pajamas. Some sleep will help with these unwanted thoughts. I'm just so tired that I'm nearly delirious. Delirium leads to horniness, right?

When I walk into the living room, hair wrapped in a towel, Maris is cleaning up her late-night snack mess.

"Thank you for doing that."

She nods. "It's the least I can do. You're feeding and helping me."

I open my mouth to respond, but a yawn escapes instead.

Maris claps her hands together. "Alright. Let's get some sleep."

I want to protest. There's much to discuss, but I can't find the energy to fight. I allow Maris to lead me to my bed, where I settle into the pillows. She leans over and looks at me with a small, tender smile. She smells of ocean breeze and citrus. So many unspoken sentiments dance in those golden eyes. I've been so focused on how Maris makes me feel that I've never stopped to think about how she feels about me.

There's the mating bond to consider, but how much does the mating bond affect your actual feelings? If there's a choice, does that mean real love can still blossom between mates?

My entire body tingles with excitement; the sensation in my chest is overwhelming.

Without thinking, I grab Maris by the back of her neck and crash her lips into mine.

Chapter 10
Alex

There's no hesitation in Maris's kiss. Where our first kiss started soft and exploratory before ramping up, this one is demanding from the start. I pull her closer until I feel her weight on top of me. Her tongue sweeps over my lips, and I open my mouth, welcoming her.

All exhaustion evaporates from me when her tongue grazes mine. A small nagging voice in the back of my mind asks me what the fuck I'm doing, but I ignore it. Maris fits too perfectly against me. How can this be wrong?

A tentacle creeps around my neck, and a breathy moan escapes my mouth. Motivated by the reaction she's elicited from me, Maris nips at my lower lip, her fangs deliciously sharp.

I shimmy and kick the blanket off me. It's suddenly too hot, and I need to be closer to Maris, with nothing between us. Tentacles assist me in the endeavor before circling up my legs, stopping right above my knees.

"Is this okay?" Maris whispers against my ear, her warm breath sending a shiver down my spine.

"Yes," I groan.

"You have to tell me what feels good," she murmurs. "Sailors are not shy with details, so I've learned a little, but this is my first time being intimate with someone."

I shouldn't be surprised that Maris is a virgin considering I was her first kiss. I angle my neck so I can look her in the eye. "Are you sure you want to do this with me?"

She frowns, brows furrowed. "Who else would I want to do this with?"

I bite my lower lip. "This is a big deal."

Maris nips at my earlobe with a sultry laugh. "You humans are so prude about sex sometimes. I promise I'm fine. Now tell me, what do you want?"

"I want you to kiss me." I tremble when her tongue circles the shell of my ear. "Just keep touching me."

She chuckles. "Are you begging, Alex?"

I do my best to glower at her but can't concentrate as another tentacle creeps up my pajama top.

Maris brushes a stray lock of hair from my face. "There's my grumpy girl."

Before I can get upset about her calling me grumpy, a tentacle brushes the bottom of my breasts. The velvety texture of her suckers against the soft, delicate skin of my breasts is unlike anything I've felt before.

My hands grip the bedsheets as I arch my stomach into her touch, silently begging for her to caress more of me. Maris obliges, not only by latching suckers onto my nipples but also by opening my legs with the tentacles that have now snaked their way up my thighs. I cry out when the suckers begin to work my nipples. I've never had both suckled at the same time, and it's incredible.

"What a beautiful sound," Maris mumbles against my neck before peppering the sensitive skin with gentle nips and kisses.

I don't know where to focus my attention. There's the tentacle stimulating my nipples and breasts; there's the one circled around my neck; there's the one that's begun to unknot my pajama bottom string; there's Maris's hands kneading and grabbing at my pliable flesh, and then there's her mouth working my collarbone. The tentacle at my pajama bottoms gives the string holding them up a final tug.

"May I?" Maris asks as the tentacle plays with the elastic waistband.

"Maris," I whine.

"Tell me what you want, Alex." She peppers each word with a kiss against the hot skin of my cheeks.

"Do it."

"Do what?" Her teeth graze my jawline.

"Whatever you want to me."

Maris smiles against my lips. "That's my girl," she purrs before plunging her tentacle inside my panties.

She feels around, obviously searching for something specific. The sailors must have told her about the anatomy of human women. I wiggle my hips, directing her to my clit.

She swallows my scream of ecstasy with her kiss when she latches onto the sensitive bundle of nerves. Her sucker works my clit in a steady rhythm as the suction on my nipples increases. Maris continues to kiss me roughly as the sensations build. My hands, previously tangled in the sheets, reach for her hair, desperate for purchase. I weave my fingers through her tresses and tug as the tentacle between my thighs sucks harder.

"Fuck!" Maris cries out as she jerks my legs farther apart. "I need to be inside you."

The tentacle down my pants unlatches itself, and I

whine at the loss. I was so close to falling over the edge. I open my mouth to protest but gasp in pleasure when the tentacle presses at the entrance of my pussy. It continues to wiggle its way in, stretching me around its increasing girth.

Maris moans into my mouth. "You feel so good. You're so tight and wet for me."

"You get off to this?" I pant.

"I told you before, my suckers are very sensitive."

She begins to move the tentacle in and out of my pussy, the texture of her suckers rubs against my walls. It feels more alien and better than any toy I've ever used alone or with a partner.

"Maris!" I groan, deep and guttural, as Maris clasps a sucker on my sweet spot at the same time one begins to suck my clit.

It's too bad time travel hasn't been invented yet because those sailors deserve a medal for teaching her about all the erogenous zones of the female body.

"You're so beautiful," Maris moans as she increases suction.

My vision goes blurry as my pleasure builds. Maris's intense golden eyes are the only thing I can see.

I writhe beneath her, and she continues to suck and thrust into me. I've never been so stimulated. Not even with my most experienced lovers. And somehow, I still want more. I buck my hips. In response, Maris slams her tentacle into me, filling me until I can't take any more of her.

Her eyes roll to the back of her head. "Alex!" Maris digs the pads of her fingers into my hips, careful not to use her sharp claws.

"Fuck! Maris! I'm going to come."

"Come for me, my grumpy girl. I need to feel that hot,

wet cunt of yours as you come." Her words are throaty as if she's struggling even to speak.

Her command is all I need. Stars flood my vision as I reach my peak. Maris throws back her head in a loud moan. Her tentacle inside me swells, and the sharp cry of her name escapes me. I'm overfilled and over-stimulated, and it's the most euphoric experience.

Maris's thrusts slow as she comes down from her orgasm. She slowly retracts her tentacle with a soft, wet pop. I let out a low moan at the loss, surprised at how empty I feel without her inside me.

With an exhausted sigh, she rolls off me but doesn't let go. Instead, all her tentacles wrap around me and pull me close until I nestle against her. I sigh into her embrace. Maris just fucked me and it was the best orgasm of my life. I want nothing more than to fall into a deep sleep.

Maris kisses the top of my head. "That was exquisite, my mate."

Uh-oh. Nope.

The moment is gone, and reality comes crashing back down. Hooking up with Maris was a bad idea. What kind of signals am I sending if one minute I don't think I want a relationship with a mythical sea monster, and the next I'm giving her an orgasm?

Wait a second. Did having sex with her just seal the mating bond?

I scramble from her embrace. "Did us fucking mean I made my choice?"

She retracts her tentacles as if I've slapped her. "No, Alex. Not at all. It just slipped. I'm sorry."

I sigh in relief, grateful I still have my choice intact. But now I've hurt Maris.

"I should be the one apologizing for the crazy mixed signals I'm sending right now."

"It's fine." Maris shrugs, looking away. "I shouldn't have touched you."

I frown. "But I'm the one who initiated it. I wanted it."

"And now you don't anymore?"

Yep. Having sex with Maris is confirmed to be a terrible idea.

"I never said that." I scowl.

How could I have been so stupid? Of course, she wants to do this more than once. I'm her fated mate. But do I want to hook up more than once? It's hard to say when I'm still wet from our encounter. I wouldn't mind having Maris inside me again, but we can't. Not until I figure out what the fuck it is I want. But how long can I string her along? She's found what she's been looking for her whole life.

I soften my features. "I'm sorry. This mate thing puts me on edge. There's just so much to consider."

"Like what?" Maris's tentacles twitch in what appears to be annoyance. "We are drawn to one another. And you liked my touch, didn't you? Or am I misreading the entire situation?"

"You're not," I snap. "But what about my choice? What about the fact that I'm a human, and you're a kraken? I know you said we wouldn't be tied unless it could work, but it makes no sense, Maris. I can't live at sea. How long before you abandon me to return to where you belong?"

She narrows her eyes. "I would never abandon you."

"Are you sure? Humans are so fragile. So many things can kill us. Are you going to freak out and destroy something when I die like you did with Thomas?"

Maris flinches. "Did you have to bring up Thomas?"

I cringe at myself, unbelieving that I went there. That was a low blow.

"I'm sorry," I say, rising from the bed. "That was real shitty of me."

"It's okay." Maris smiles softly. "Emotions are high right now."

I get up and walk towards the bedroom door.

"Where are you going?"

The concern in her voice hurts my stomach.

"You're right," I explain. "Emotions are high. We both need to cool off."

"Let me guess." Her voice is bitter. "You're going to sleep somewhere else?"

I nod. "It's for the best."

"I understand." Maris frowns and turns her face away, refusing to look me in the eyes.

With a twinge of regret, I close the door behind me with a soft click.

Chapter 11
Maris

Asoft knock gently wakes me from my fitful sleep. I've been churning over everything that happened yesterday all night long. I had my mate in my embrace, and I fucked it up. She orgasmed, my name on her lips, and she left me alone in this cold, empty bed. There's a part of me that wishes she didn't kiss me because I will never be satisfied now that I've been inside her.

Alex is magnificent. The fates blessed me by tying us together. A kraken couldn't ask for a more perfect mate. Yet, she doesn't want me, and the moon grows fuller by the day. I can't pressure her to make a choice. If she doesn't hate me already, she definitely would if I forced her hand.

Disturbing my mate is the last thing I want to do right now. She would feel guilty if she knew I was this upset over our encounter.

"Come in," I rasp, my throat sore from crying.

Alex opens the door a crack and peeks through. "I came to talk about the next steps of our plan."

I wave her in. "I've been thinking."

She smiles. "Me too. Hopefully, we're on the same page with what to do next."

I shake my head. "I think I should do this alone." It pains me to suggest separating. But Alex being away from me for a few days might give her the space she needs to decide.

Her eyes widen. "What do you mean?"

"You've been an excellent help, Alex. And there's no way I would be this far without you, but may I be honest?"

Alex nods, chewing her lower lip.

"After last night, I worry this situation is stressful for you. Maybe you need a few days to yourself."

She looks wide-eyed, as if I've slapped her in the face. "Are you serious right now?"

I startle at her words. Shouldn't she feel relieved I'm offering her an out? "I beg your pardon?"

Alex pinches her nose and takes a deep breath. "I'm sorry. That wasn't the appropriate reaction. I can see how you would jump to this conclusion. But I just don't appreciate being told how I should feel rather than being asked."

How could I be so clueless? Of course, the woman who wants to decide for herself would also like her thoughts and emotions respected. As her mate, I should know better.

"I'm sorry, Alex." I cringe. "I made an unfair assumption."

Her expression softens. "I appreciate you looking out for me, but I'll let you know if I need a break."

"Understood." I grin, rising from the bed. "Can we have breakfast while we discuss the plan?"

"We don't have time." Alex tosses me a can of tuna and a fork. "Ella is on her way to pick us up. She's grabbing food on her way, but I figure you might need a snack."

"Ella?" I perk up. "Your best friend?"

"Yes." Alex grins wide. "You're going to love her."

I gobble the tuna in one bite, eager to meet my mate's best friend. "I can't wait."

"Great!" Alex claps her hands. "Let's get ready! I laid out your dresses on the guest-room bed."

Alex and I head in different directions to get ready. I check the mirror for any tangles in my hair and brush my teeth with the spare toothbrush Alex gave me, which I have to admit is a delightful sensation. Just as I'm laying out a pink dress to change into, the doorbell rings.

The urge to run out and greet Ella is strong, but I hang back since I'm still in my kraken form. I have no idea what Ella knows about me or my situation with Alex. There's no need giving my mate's best friend a heart attack.

I close my eyes, preparing to transform, when there's a knock on my door.

"One second!" I call out.

"It's okay, Maris. I told Ella everything," Alex answers back.

I crack open the door. "Everything?"

"Yes."

A thrill shivers through me. My mate actually told her best friend about me? Alex may not have accepted me yet, but this has got to count as a step in the right direction.

When I fling open the bedroom door, my breath is stolen from chest when I lay eyes on the angelic visage of Ella.

An intricate design of braids starts at her hairline before ending at the crown of her head in a cloud of tight inky-black ringlets. Dark freckles dot Ella's tawny-brown skin, pairing perfectly with her round and delicate features. I expect her to hold herself confidently, considering her beauty and height, which almost reaches my human form.

Instead, she shrinks as if she's taking up too much space, her eyes wide. She must be shy.

But I've already decided we're going to be great friends. "Ella!" I pull her in for a tight hug.

"Oh." Ella pats my back as I embrace her. "It's nice to meet you."

I give her one more tight squeeze before releasing her.

"I...uhh..." Ella stares at me, mouth agape.

Alex's brow creases. "Are you okay, Ella?"

Ella swallows, throat bobbing. "I know you said Maris is a kraken, but I didn't really believe you."

"You thought I made it up?"

"No!" Ella fidgets with the hem of her dress. "I thought *you* believed you met a kraken maybe, and that Maris was just a really weird chick."

Alex chuckles. "And you were going to help us anyway?"

"What are friends for?" Ella shrugs.

I beam, loving Ella already for how supportive she is of my mate. "I appreciate that you're willing to help."

Ella coughs. "Of course. Um...one more thing?"

Alex nods. "Anything."

"Can I touch a tentacle? I just need to make sure this isn't some elaborate costume."

"Ella!" Alex gasps.

I laugh. "It's no big deal." I extend a tentacle toward Ella, who grazes the tip with her fingers.

"Yeap. That's real." She points down the hall. "If you don't mind, I'm gonna take a few moments to process this, preferably on the couch."

Alex takes Ella by the elbow. "That's totally fine. Maris still needs to transform and get dressed anyway."

After I finish getting ready by changing into my human

form and getting dressed, I meet Alex and Ella on the couch. Ella eyes me, mouth twisted into a frown.

"Are you feeling any better, Ella?" I ask.

"I'm still freaking out a little, if I'm being honest," she admits, standing up and smoothing her dress. "But I can't waste any more time."

Alex rubs her back. "That's my girl!"

I smile. "I'm happy to answer any questions you have."

Alex snatches a banana off the counter and begins to peel it. "Ask in the car. I don't want to miss the ferry."

I blanch when she bites into the fruit. Even the smell is too sweet.

Alex rolls her eyes. "When will you get over your weird thing with bananas?"

"When they stop being so disgusting." I stick my tongue out.

Ella motions to the bag Alex is carrying. "Is this your overnight bag? I'll take it."

"Yes." Alex hands it to Ella. "Thank you."

I follow them out of the door. "Overnight bag? What's happening?"

"I'll explain in the car," she says as she locks the front door.

Ella loads the bag into the backseat of her vehicle. I squeal in excitement. I've never been in a car before! I wonder how different it is than a moped.

Alex chuckles. "Do you want to sit in the front seat?"

I weigh my options. Ella slides into the left side behind what looks like a tiny helm, which I assume is where she controls the vehicle. If I sit next to her, that puts Alex in the back by herself.

"I want to sit next to you," I say finally, chin lifted.

Alex's nose crinkles. "But Ella is driving."

"We can sit behind her together."

"Uh…that's weird. Ella isn't a chauffeur."

Ella lets out a musical laugh. "It's okay, Alex. If your mate wants to sit next to you, she can."

Alex's cheeks flush a bright red as she glowers. "Are you going to give me shit about this too?"

"Of course!" Ella beams. "Especially when your mate is as pretty as Maris."

"Whatever," Alex mumbles. She turns to me. "We can sit in the backseat together."

With an excited yelp, I jump into the seat behind Ella. A mouth-watering aroma hits me as soon as I'm in the car. I recognize eggs, but the greasy scent is unknown to me.

"Why does your car smell so delicious?" My mouth waters despite having already consumed a can of tuna.

"It's breakfast." Ella smiles as she digs through a grease-stained paper bag. She hands me a warm bundle wrapped in parchment paper about the size of my fist. "I hope you like bacon."

I sniff the package. "What is it?"

"A bacon, egg, and cheese bagel sandwich. They make their bagels fresh."

Alex grabs her sandwich from Ella, unwraps it, and immediately takes a large bite. She throws her head back with a contented groan.

My eyes widen. The sounds of satisfaction Alex makes while she eats the sandwich are dangerously similar to the ones she made when I pleasured her, except not as uninhib-ited. My tentacles twitch under my glamor, eager to make her moan again. But I take a few calming breaths instead. The last thing I need is to transform because Alex's noises arouse me.

"Betty's Best Bagels is my favorite," she says through a full mouth.

Going off her previous favorite foods, I'm inclined to turn it down but it does smell delicious. I unwrap the paper and waft in the smell of melty cheese and runny egg before taking a large bite. The salty bacon adds a crispy texture to the gooey mess, while the bagel sops up the grease. No wonder Alex acted like this sandwich is orgasmic. I scarf it down in three bites. It's so delicious. Maybe even more so than pizza.

Ella stares at me, mouth agape. "Um...we aren't even out of the driveway."

Alex doesn't even look at me. "You'll get used to it."

"Alright." Ella chuckles awkwardly. "Let's hit the road. It shouldn't take us long to get there, but it is on the other side of the island."

The car is smoother than the moped, but I miss wrapping my arms around Alex and pressing myself against her back. However, talking and listening to music during the ride is nice. Ella was amenable to turning on Disney Princess music.

During the drive, Alex explains the plan. "The Bermuda Triangle starts right outside Miami. Ella's dad lives in Miami and owns a boat. He was kind enough to let us borrow it. We're taking a ferry to Miami because Sunshine Key is kind of a weird outlier of The Keys. The ferry is faster and more direct than the overseas highway."

I nod along. Alex's plan makes sense.

She continues, "We can ride out towards Bermuda for about a day. I figure that will be far enough out to summon your father. Hopefully, he can fill in the blanks of what happened to you." She looks at me expectantly. "What do you think?"

I beam with pride. My mate is so smart. "If it doesn't work, I don't know what will."

"Alex is a great planner," Ella interjects from the front seat. "I guess that's why she's such a good pool manager."

Alex snorts. "I'm sure Carter disagrees right about now. I asked him to cover my shifts until I get back."

"He'll get over it." Ella rolls her eyes, her tone biting. "He's such a jerk."

"You only say that because he's your ex."

My jaw drops. "You dated Carter?"

Ella nods. "And it fucking sucked." She covers her mouth with her hand. "Pardon my language."

Alex leans forward to place a hand on Ella's shoulder. "It's okay. He was a complete tool to you. I would have fired him if you had let me."

"Thanks, Alex." Ella rests her head on Alex's hand. "But that would have been unethical. I couldn't let you risk your job for me."

My heart swells as I observe the tender moment. Alex loves her sister, but that bond is more about Avery taking care of Alex. The friendship between Alex and Ella has equal footing. I can tell they've loved each other for a long time. Seeing my mate like this makes me fall harder for her.

Traffic becomes denser as we travel through a part of the island with more buildings. People crowd the sidewalks, many carrying large bags similar to the one Alex brought but on wheels. The hustle and bustle reminds me of being back on Thomas's pirate ship, but without the organization.

"Are we getting close?" I ask, pressing my nose against the window.

"Yes! Most of these people are tourists. It looks like the

ferry will be a little crowded today," Alex answers. "Hopefully, we can find a quiet spot."

Ella anchors the car in front of a large pier leading to a massive boat. "The tourists will congregate on the lower deck where they won't get as queasy."

Alex turns towards me, her forehead creased in concern. "Do you get seasick?"

I shoot her a quizzical look.

She buries her face in her hands. "Of course, you don't get seasick."

"I appreciate you double-checking." I use my hand to stifle my giggle, not wanting Alex to feel embarrassed for caring.

Ella turns around in her seat. "You two better get going if you want to grab a beer before the ferry sets sail."

Alex scrambles out of the car. "Oh no! I can't miss out on that cheap, shitty beer."

I follow her to the trunk. "Why would we want to drink shitty beer?"

"Because it's the best kind," she says with a beaming smile as she slings the bag over her shoulder.

Ella sticks her head out of the window. "Text me when you're on the way home, and I'll pick you up."

"Sounds good." Alex waves to her as she heads towards the ferry.

I can't help but reach through the car window and wrap my arms around Ella's neck for a tight embrace.

"You are quite the hugger, aren't you?" Her mouth presses against my shoulder, muffling her question.

I let her go. "Yes! Especially with my friends."

Ella frowns, her brows furrowed. "We're friends?"

"Of course!"

She offers me a soft smile. "I'll see you in a few days."

I offer one last winning grin before racing after Alex.

Alex passes me a cold can of beer when we reach the ferry's top deck. "Thank you for being so kind to Ella."

"I adore her already."

She sighs. "Ella is a wonderful person, but she's so painfully shy. We met in kindergarten and have been inseparable since. I often wonder if me being her only friend is holding her back."

I shake my head. "How is that a bad thing? You're an amazing friend. What more could she ask for?"

Alex shrugs. "I'm a solitary introvert. I'm happy only having Ella and Avery, and now you. But Ella? I know she wants more and I often wonder if she wants a partner. She's only dated Carter and that was a disaster."

"You'll have to trust that she'll find romance when ready."

"You're right." Alex takes a long swig of beer before nodding towards mine. "Are you going to try it?"

I sniff the yeasty aroma, soothed by the scent. When the cool, bubbly liquid hits my tongue, memories rush back to me. Thomas loved a frothy beer with a slab of salty beef and a side of oranges. Despite my massive appetite, he always ensured there was enough at the table to feed me. A tear rolls down my cheek, and I scrub it away.

Alex places a hand on my shoulder. "Are you okay?"

"I remembered more about Thomas. Beer was his favorite."

"Do you miss him?"

I nod. "Incredibly."

"I can't imagine losing Ella or Avery. It must hurt."

"It does." I grimace. "Thomas would be so disappointed in me if he knew I destroyed his ship. He never intended for me to mourn him like that."

Alex pulls me into her, burying her head against my shoulder. "It's okay. You couldn't have predicted how you would react to your grief."

"But I put everyone in danger." My bottom lip wobbles as I hold back the urge to sob. "His ship and crew were the most important things in Thomas's life, and I destroyed them both."

As if Alex knows what I need without asking, she's silent. There's nothing she can say to make it better, but her touch is enough to soothe the ache. I wonder what Thomas would think of her. He would probably dote on her, adoring her grumpy exterior but soft interior.

Alex lets me cry silent tears. This experience of slowly regaining my traumatizing memories should be alienating, and it would be if it weren't for my mate. I don't feel alone when she's near. Even if she rejects me, these precious moments with her will be my most treasured.

Our quiet is interrupted by the clamoring of our fellow passengers. We are no longer alone on the top deck. I sigh, stepping away from Alex, and attempt to regain my composure. She takes a long look at me before reaching up, taking my face in her hands, and wiping away my tears with her thumbs.

The moment is over too soon when one of the passengers lets out a loud whoop, followed by a burst of drunken laughter.

Alex rolls her eyes. "It's not even 10 a.m."

"They're having fun." I nudge her with my elbow. "Maybe you should let loose a little."

"What do you mean?" She scowls.

"We're on a boat! There's nothing else to do! Bottom's up!" I chug the rest of my beer and crush the can.

Alex looks at me, mouth agape. Is she going to go for this?

Her look of disbelief morphs into a large smile. "Alright! Let's do it!"

I cheer as Alex finishes her drink.

We spend the rest of the ferry ride drinking beer and talking about anything and everything. I learn about Alex's life growing up on Sunshine Key with Ella and Avery, how she discovered her passion for interior decorating, and her dream of adopting a senior cat.

"Why haven't you adopted a cat yet?" I cock my head. "Thomas had one he loved very much named Mister Tibs. They make excellent companions."

"Mister...Tibs?" Alex slurs the question. She can't hold her alcohol as well as I can, but I'm a magical being. It takes a lot to get me drunk.

I beam. "Yes. He was the best little baby man."

"I don't know what a little baby man is," she says, quirking an eyebrow.

"You'll know when you see one," I explain with a wink.

Alex stumbles to the ferry railing to look over the horizon. "You're right, Maris. Why not adopt a cat?"

I chuckle. "I can't think of a reason."

She gasps and starts jumping up and down. "Let's go to the shelter when we get back!"

Her look of pure hope and excitement sends a thrill through me. I could deny her nothing.

Alex's expression sobers. "But what if you decide to stay with your dad?"

My stomach drops. I've already told her I would never leave her. But this drunk side of Alex must be bringing out all her doubts and worries, even the ones I thought I had quelled. I need to do better. It's time to stop playing coy. There are only a few more days left for her to decide if she wants to be with me, so why am I holding back?

I wrap an arm around her waist and pull her hips against me. Alex looks up at me, her eyes glinting with hope.

I lean down, pressing my lips to the shell of her ear. "I would never leave you."

She sighs into my embrace. "But you belong in the sea."

"I belong with you."

I pull back so I can gaze into her beautiful hazel eyes. Alex closes them and rocks onto her toes. Her lips part, seeking mine. But I can't bring myself to kiss her. Instead, I press my lips to her forehead. She's drunk. Not only is it wrong to take advantage, but an inebriated choice is not the same as a sober choice.

A pout forms on her mouth when she realizes I won't kiss her. I hold back a giggle. Her petulance is adorable.

I twirl a lock of Alex's hair in my finger, enjoying the silky texture. "Don't worry, my grumpy girl. If you still want me to kiss you when you're sober, I'll ravish you."

Her cheeks turn a bright pink. "Maris—"

"I spy Miami!" one of our fellow drunk passengers squeals, pointing across the horizon to a cluster of jagged vertical blocks I recognize as skyscrapers from watching TV with Alex and Avery.

Excitement buzzes through me. The tallest building

I've ever seen is a lighthouse, so I look forward to seeing these towering structures up close. Alex spends the rest of the ride struggling to recall facts about Miami. She settles on naming her favorite places to eat and shop for home goods.

As we approach the city, I begin to sweat. Skyscrapers are much taller than lighthouses. It's a bit of a wake-up call to see how far humanity has advanced in 200 years. No wonder Alex struggled with the whole kraken thing. How can humans believe in magic when technology has propelled them so far?

Alex slips her hand in mine, a soft smile on her face. Her touch instantly calms me. Our mating bond must be growing stronger. I don't have to express my needs verbally, she just knows.

When we dock at the pier, passengers file to the various exits. Alex and I hang back. She's still drunk, and I want to make getting off the ferry as easy as possible. Once most of the passengers have cleared from the boat, I offer myself as stability for Alex. We manage to exit with minimal stumbles.

"Alex! Hey! Over here!" A handsome gentleman with dark umber skin and close-cropped gray hair jogs towards us.

"Bryan!" Alex launches herself into the man's arms.

"Whoa!" His deep brown eyes sparkle as he laughs. "Are you drunk?"

"Maybe a little." Alex turns to me. "Bryan, this is Maris. Maris, this is Bryan. He's basically my second dad."

Bryan ruffles Alex's hair. "I tell everyone I have three daughters. You, Ella, and Avery."

"Avery!" Alex stomps her foot. "I better be your favorite."

He tilts his head back and roars with jolly laughter. "I forgot how bratty you get when you drink."

I hold out my hand for Bryan to shake. "It's kind of cute, though."

"Is this the first time you've seen her like this?" He offers me a genuine smile as he takes my hand.

"It is."

"You're a good girlfriend if you think this side of Alex is cute." He lets go of my hand. "And a strong handshake! I like that in a person."

I glance at Alex, expecting her to freak over the 'girlfriend' comment, but instead, she just smiles at me. She must have told Bryan we're dating since it'd be easier to explain that than the truth, which is fine by me. The less people that know I'm a kraken, the better. Besides, I look forward to pretending to date Alex. The closer I can get to my mate, the better.

Bryan grabs our bag and leads us to his 'truck,' an even larger car. Something about the vehicle feels familiar, but I can't quite put a finger on why. It makes me uneasy. I shake away my discomfort. There's no time for this.

The drive to his home is filled with Alex's bubbly chatter about the pool and redesigning her house. Bryan offers tips for renovating the outside, and Alex nods along, typing notes into her phone. By the time we reach our destination, Alex has sobered a little.

"Are you ladies hungry?" Bryan asks as he anchors his vehicle.

"So hungry," Alex groans. "Are you making steaks?"

He laughs. "Of course. Maris, how do you like your steak?"

I shrug. "I've never had it."

Bryan opens his mouth, but Alex cuts him off, "She's from Europe."

He nods as if that explains everything. "There's one problem with this. I'm going to ruin all steak for you."

Alex licks her lips. "Bryan cooks beef to perfection."

When we walk through the front door, Bryan gives us a pained smile. "I only have one spare bed. But I figured since you were dating, it's not a big deal for you to share a room."

Alex freezes, horror apparent on her face. Thankfully, Bryan is too busy carrying our bag down the hall to notice.

I lean down to whisper in Alex's ear. "It will be okay. We'll figure something out." We could put pillows between us or something.

She nods, her shoulders relaxing. "That's fine," she calls after Bryan.

"Excellent," he remarks, returning from the guest room. "Maris, would you like a tour?"

I follow Bryan around his home, marveling at how different it is from Alex's. Alex decorated her house in bright, comforting colors; Bryan's is primarily gray with minimal adornments besides a few framed photos of Ella.

After the quick tour, Bryan leads us to the backyard and fires up his grill. We spend the rest of the evening conversing and eating. The steaks are indeed fantastic, along with the roasted potatoes. I don't dare try the fruit salad, letting Alex devour almost the entire bowl.

Bryan is an endearing man who's excited we're taking his boat on an adventure. I learn over the course of the evening that Alex told him she wanted to take me on a memorable trip to celebrate our anniversary. Thankfully, Bryan doesn't press us for details. He just offers us a knowing smile when Alex thanks him for letting us borrow his boat.

I worry Bryan will pick up on the fact that Alex and I aren't girlfriends, but our chemistry is so easy that he never shows suspicion. Alex puts her hand on mine, shoots me lingering looks, and giggles at all my jokes. To an outsider, we look smitten with each other. The fact that I'm totally taken by her probably helps sell the illusion.

Bryan heaves himself off his chair when the sun finally dips below the horizon. "The summer sun sets so late. I don't mean to be the old man, but we should probably get to bed if you want an early launch tomorrow morning."

Alex nods, and we follow him inside. He asks if we need anything, and when we decline, he shuffles up the stairs to his bedroom, leaving Alex and me alone. She looks everywhere but at me as we approach the guest room.

She sucks in a sharp inhale when she opens the door. The bed against the center wall is small, too small for two people to comfortably share without touching. We couldn't even put pillows between us. If we want to share this bed, we will have to press against each other.

Oh no. What are we going to do?

Chapter 12
Alex

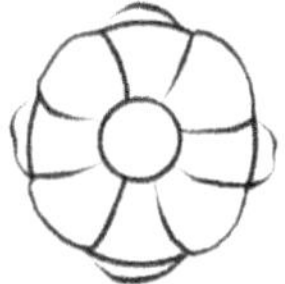

When Bryan said there was only one bed, I assumed it was at least a queen. We could have just slept on the opposite edges of the bed, but there's no way we can both fit without getting cozy. I glance at Maris to see how she feels, but her face is annoyingly neutral.

Ella would be in hysterics if she were here. As an avid romance book reader, she never hesitates to fill me in on various tropes and cliches, and Maris and I are living one right now.

Wait.

Would we also classify as fake dating since we technically lied to Bryan about our relationship? But we didn't have to pretend to have feelings. Maris and I casually touched and flirted throughout the day. It was easy and natural.

But now I'm alone with her and this one bed dilemma with all our romantic and sexual tension. I hope Maris will eagerly accept that we must share, and I can snuggle with her guilt-free. As selfish of me as it is, I want to be intimate without sending her mixed signals.

Instead of welcoming our predicament, Maris twirls a dark green lock around her finger, deep in thought. *Shit.* Of course, she is trying to come up with a solution. After I practically ran away from her last night, she must think I hate her.

"I can sleep on the floor," Maris finally suggests.

"No way!"

Even if I weren't secretly hoping Maris would have to cuddle me, I would never allow someone I care about to sleep on the ground.

"I'll be okay." Maris shrugs. "I used to sleep in the sand, remember? Just toss me a pillow, and I'll be comfortable."

"That's not fair to you."

"It's also not fair for you to be put in a situation you aren't comfortable with."

I cringe. "Maris, sharing a bed with you would not be uncomfortable."

She stiffens. "I'm not sure this is a good idea."

"Why not?"

"Because"—she turns to face me—"I don't think I could handle it if you change your mind."

I'm such a shithead. Maris must be confused by my actions, and I don't blame her. Sleeping with her fucked things up. The only way to fix it is to be consistent and make my choice about being her mate. Maybe it's time to be honest so she knows where I stand.

"Maris." I take her hands in mine. "I'm still confused about the mate thing, but I know you're special to me. I want to explore a relationship with you, but there are so many questions and doubts surrounding how we would even be together considering you're a kraken and I'm just a mere human. And then there's my stubborn streak. I want to be sure we care about each other for real and not just because of some fated bond."

Her eyes search mine. Will she accept my truth? Or will she pull away? The most challenging aspect of being vulnerable is the potential rejection. If she does dismiss me, I wouldn't blame her. Do I even deserve Maris's acceptance after the emotional roller coaster I've put her through?

"How about this?" Maris finally breaks the deafening silence. "I desperately need water, and you probably want to bathe, right?"

Is she about to suggest we take a shower together? Surely not. That would be even more tempting than sharing a bed, right? I have to admit, I'm intrigued.

I raise my eyebrows and nod. Where is Maris going with this?

She chuckles. "I'm not suggesting we get naked together."

"Oh." Despite my best efforts, I can't help the disappointed tone in my voice.

"Don't tempt me," she whispers, tucking my hair behind my ears. "Use the opportunity to think about this while you bathe. Then, while I'm soaking, you can consider some more. Because here's the deal, Alex, you share a bed with me, I won't let you go until the sun rises."

I swallow thickly. Sleeping with Maris wrapped around me sounds delightful. But she's right. I need to think it through before I cause us both heartache.

Maris suggests I shower before she soaks since it might take some time for the itching to stop. I hate leaving her alone with burning skin, but I appreciate her consideration of me. As I wash the day's adventures away, my mind wanders to all the thoughtful things Maris has done.

She's taken care of me while I was drunk, protected me

from the mermaid, was kind to Ella, befriended my sister, and has not pressured me into making any decisions. Maris is careful with how she handles me and is now going out of her way to make sure I'm comfortable.

The more I think about it, the more I doubt my resolve. What am I fighting this for? Whoever pulls the strings paired me with someone who makes me feel cared for and beautiful. I've never experienced this kind of security before. Do I dare say that I feel loved?

The last person who made me feel loved besides my family was Ella. But this is different. Ella is my best friend. The comforting, platonic love I have for her is vastly different from the alluring pull to Maris. I can't believe I just used 'love' when thinking about Maris. It's daunting and unknown, but it makes the most sense.

Is it possible to love someone after meeting them a few days ago? Logically, my brain revolts against the idea. But the pitter-pattering in my chest says otherwise. I've heard of whirlwind romances where couples get married almost immediately and then spend the rest of their long lives together, happy and content. Why couldn't that be me and Maris? Granted, we have the immortal versus mortal thing going against us, but as Maris said, we wouldn't be fated if we couldn't work.

I finish my shower quickly, eager to get Maris in the water. When I enter the bedroom, which is thankfully attached to the guest room, Maris is back in her kraken form. But she looks awful. Her usual bright skin has turned a dull blue, and her tentacles writhe weakly.

"Oh god, Maris!" I rush to her side, letting go of the towel I have wrapped around myself. "We need to get you in water now."

"I'll be okay." Maris stumbles as she tries to wave me off.

I loop my arm through hers. It's awkward because she's almost two feet taller than me in kraken form, but it at least gives her some support. Together, we limp to the bathroom. Well, I wouldn't call Maris's struggle to move 'limping.' It's more like she's dragging herself across the floor.

"Where's the tub?" Maris asks when we finally reach the bathroom.

Bryan's guest ensuite has a shower stall rather than a tub. I hadn't considered this problem, but maybe soaking her in the water stream will be enough.

"The water pressure is pretty impressive. Let's try this first before coming up with a plan B." I turn on the faucet before helping Maris heave herself into the shower.

She lets out a long sigh of relief after allowing the water to pelt her for a few moments. "Thank you. I feel better already."

Thank goodness that worked. I didn't feel like sneaking out of Bryan's to find a larger body of water. That could have been disastrous. Imagine explaining Maris to Bryan or a random neighbor of his. It's not even close to Halloween, so we'd be kind of fucked.

I observe Maris for a moment to ensure the color returns to her skin. When a chill breeze from the air vent raises goosebumps on my arms, I hug myself tight. *Oh shit. I'm still naked.* I dropped my towel in my rush to help Maris.

She has never seen me naked, which is a little crazy to think about since she gave me the best orgasm of my life. I got over my insecurities about my thick body in my mid-twenties, but that doesn't mean I'm comfortable being seen without clothes.

I duck out of the bathroom and throw on my pajamas.

Maris asked me to consider sharing a bed while she's in the shower. Honestly, feelings aside, I can't imagine forcing her to sleep on the hardwood floor after this ordeal.

The bed is piled high with decorative pillows in various shades of rust. It's not my vibe, but I still respect Bryan's attempt at adding color to this room. I stack the unnecessary bedding on the floor before fluffing the comforter. This bed needs to be as comfortable as possible for Maris.

My heart rate picks up when the steady stream of the shower dies. Should I already be in bed waiting for her? Or will it look like I expect her to be on the floor? I need to decide quickly, but indecision freezes me. Story of my life.

"Are you alright?" Maris asks, entering the bedroom.

I startle out of my racing thoughts. "Uh...yes. Are you ready for bed?"

Her golden eyes bore into me, her expression inscrutable. "Are you sure you want to do this?"

"I'm sure." I peel back the comforter and slide into the bed. "Come on," I encourage, patting the space beside me.

A contented grin spreads across her beautiful face. When did I grow to love that smile so much?

Maris crawls in next to me. The tiny bed creaks and groans, and I roll into her when it sags beneath her weight. My hands can't help but roam over her velvety skin, still damp from her shower. She feels incredible, but then she winces at my touch.

"I'm sorry." I flinch, dropping my hands.

"Your touch feels nice. Too nice. My tentacles..." Maris says through clenched teeth.

I look down and giggle. Her tentacles are circling in on themselves, clearly fighting the urge to wrap around me.

"Maris?"

"Yes, Alex?" Her eyes shut tight.

"Will you hold me?"

Instantly, two tentacles snake up each leg while two more wrap around my waist, pulling me against her as the little spoon to her big spoon. One of Maris's arms drapes over me, while the other squirms its way beneath, encircling me. Being in her embrace is like being in the world's best heated and weighted blanket.

I wiggle to get even more comfortable, and when I let out a satisfied sigh, Maris buries her face in my still-damp hair with a happy hum. The bedside lamp clicks off, I assume by one of Maris's free tentacles. In the dark, I can focus on the subtlety of her. From her breathing to the occasional gentle squeeze of her tentacles, Maris provides constant and soothing reminders that she's with me.

When her breathing becomes deep and steady, I know she's fallen asleep. I bring one of her hands to my lips and press gentle kisses against her skin. Maris lets out a soft sigh but doesn't wake. My heart swells. I have missed out by not cuddling with her every night since I brought her home. I will never make that mistake again. This is the coziest I've ever been.

"I'm falling in love with you, Maris," I whisper to the dark.

It doesn't respond, and neither does Maris. That's fine. I'm getting sleepy anyway. It's not long before the combination of her steady breathing and comforting embrace lulls me into a deep, dreamless sleep.

A soft knock gently wakes me from my slumber.

"Alex? Maris? We need to get going." The closed door muffles Bryan's voice.

I try to roll over, but Maris has me securely wrapped in her warm embrace. *Oh shit!* If Bryan opens the door, he'll see Maris as a kraken. I squirm until the tentacles loosen so I can face her.

"Maris?" I whisper as I poke her in the cheek. "You need to change."

She mumbles something incoherent. The only thing I catch is "my mate." It would be cute, but there's an urgent issue in the shape of a middle-aged man at the door.

"Girls?" Bryan calls again, followed by a more insistent knock.

"Be out in a minute!" I call back.

This time, my gentle poke is more of an aggressive prod. "Maris. Wake up."

Maris's eyes flutter open. When her eyes finally focus on me, she offers me a wide, sleepy smile. "Good morning, Alex."

I can't help but grin back. "Good morning, sleepyhead."

She hums and tightens her tentacles around me.

"No!" I wriggle away from her with a laugh. "We have to get up. Bryan is waiting for us."

"Boo!" She pouts.

I tickle her sides. "Come on! I'm eager to get started."

Maris groans but unwinds her tentacles and rolls out of bed. "Yes, ma'am."

We get ready in a comfortable silence. I steal glances at Maris occasionally, and every time I do, she's looking right back at me. The fact that I had the best sleep of my life while cuddling Maris is not lost on me. There's something special about her, about us.

I've never been vulnerable with someone like I was last night with Maris. She accepted me and made me feel safe. It's frustrating because I want to continue our conversation, but we can't. Instead, we're rushing to meet Bryan and get on a boat. It will have to wait.

Bryan is waiting for us in his rooster-themed breakfast nook, several totes crammed full of stuff scattered at his feet. "This is all the supplies you'll need. You said you'd only be gone for three days at most, but I packed you enough for a week. Just in case."

I fling my arms around his neck. "Thank you, Bryan! I appreciate you shopping for us. Let me know how much I owe you."

"Nonsense!" He waves me off. "I never get to spoil you girls anymore."

"That's because we're not girls! We're all in our thirties." I hide a smile behind my hand. Bryan misses his daughter.

Ella's mom filed for divorce when she was only eight and did everything in her power to cut him off. He fought tooth and nail to visit Ella, but it wasn't until she turned eighteen that she was able to have the relationship she really wanted with him. Since he didn't get to see her much until she was an adult, to him, we are still kids. Whenever he visits, or Ella and I make the trip to see him, he overindulges us.

"That may be true, but you should still let me do this for you."

"Alright." I roll my eyes, smiling. "I'll allow it."

"I appreciate it, Bryan." Maris nods.

After gathering the supply bags, we pile into Bryan's truck and drive to the marina. Maris begs him to play Disney music, but he insists on jamming to dad rock. She doesn't mind. In fact, by the time we reach our destination, Maris is singing along with the punk rock crooners. She doesn't know the words, but she tries anyway. As I watch her, I become more sure of my feelings for her.

"Do you have your boating license on you?" Bryan asks as we finish loading the boat.

It's a gorgeous pontoon boat with a cabin large enough for a king-sized bed, toilet and shower, a small kitchen, and a table for eating meals. He uses it for overnight fishing trips with his buddies, but we will use it for the next few days to track down the most feared creature in the sea.

I fish it out of my bag to show him. "Of course! You think I would forget it after the grief you put me, Ella, and Avery through to take that boating course?"

Bryan laughs. "Always so testy! But you live on an island! You need to know how to drive a boat!"

Maris throws an arm around my shoulders. "What else do you expect from this grumpy girl?"

I attempt to glower at her but end up smiling instead. There's just something about how Maris calls me 'grumpy girl' that turns me into a smiling goof. Maybe it's the way she said it when she fucked me the other night.

Now is *not* the time to be thinking about how amazing her tentacle felt inside me, or how good the sucker felt on my nipples, or even the way she moaned my name.

"It's good to see you so happy, Alex," Bryan says, clapping his hand on my shoulder, interrupting my naughty thoughts.

His comment makes me smile. Despite my life turning upside down since rescuing Maris, it's been for the better. I want to tell her all these things, but all I can do for the moment is lean into her. She squeezes me against her. I love Bryan, but I can't wait to be alone with my kraken.

The plan is to cruise east at a moderate speed for a day. We hope it will be far enough into the Bermuda Triangle to summon Caspian. Thankfully, Bryan has the most state-of-the-art navigation system on top of laminated maps. There's no way we're getting lost.

As I drive, Maris tells me what she can remember about her life and father. She has no memories of a mother. While her parents were bonded mates and Caspian was madly in love with Maris's mother, her mother had feelings for a sea nymph. Once Maris was born, her mother left Maris in the care of Caspian before stealing away with her lover, never to be seen again, only occasionally felt through the bond by her father.

My heart leaps as Maris tells me the story of her mother. Not only did she exercise her choice to not be with Caspian, but she chose to be with the one she really loves. Despite this revelation confirming Maris's declaration that we have a choice, I can't help but feel the heavy tug of melancholy in my chest. To bond with your mate and then have them leave you? That must be soul-crushing.

I already feel such a strong connection to Maris, and I haven't even accepted the bond. As stubborn as I have been about making everything my choice, the truth is that I've been ignoring the fact that Maris is special to me.

Maris is back in her kraken form, having transformed as soon as we were out of eyesight of the marina. Whenever we pass another boat, she simply ducks into the cabin. We only pause for sunscreen application, restroom breaks, and a lunch of sandwiches. It's another perfect day with Maris.

We finally decide to anchor for the night as the sun begins its descent below the horizon. There aren't any boats within view. The vast emptiness of the ocean's surface is both eerie and beautiful. But I know underneath, the water is teeming with life. And not just the creatures we see on the *Discovery Channel*, but the stuff of legends.

As I baste salmon steaks with butter and garlic, I get lost in thoughts of Maris. I'm nervous to meet Caspian. Will he be able to help? What if he doesn't like me? I groan at my pathetic need to be liked. When was the last time I gave a shit about what someone thought of me? It's not like Maris is my girlfriend yet, so I shouldn't be freaking out.

"What's the matter?" Maris asks, appearing at my side. She's dripping wet from her soak in the ocean.

"Just thinking about your father," I admit.

"What about him?" She squeezes my hip. "That smells heavenly, by the way."

Her touch is gone too soon, but it still causes my heart rate to speed up. "Thank you. And I'm just nervous about meeting him."

Maris begins rifling through the cabinets, looking for dishes and cutlery so she can set the small table. "Are you worried he won't like you?"

"No!" I cringe, heat creeping up my neck, too embarrassed to tell Maris the truth.

She laughs. "You are!"

"Fine!" I'm a terrible liar. "I'm scared he'll hate me."

Her arms encircle my waist from behind, and she buries her face in my hair. "It'll be okay."

I lean into Maris, pressing my ass against her. All my worries melt away as I become instantly turned on by having her body against mine. It's not that we didn't touch today. In fact, we couldn't keep our hands off each other, but it was casual, comforting, and family-friendly. This is the first time Maris's touch has been sexually intimate.

A low groan emits from the back of her throat. "Alex." Her tentacles wrap around my ankles.

"Yes?" My voice is breathy.

"Please don't tease me."

"Who said I'm teasing?" I ask with a throaty chuckle.

Maris spins me around so I'm facing her. Her eyes glint with dark desire. My knees nearly buckle under her lustful gaze.

"What do you want from me?" she growls.

I narrow my eyes, intent on being honest with her and what I want. "I want you to fuck me."

Chapter 13
Maris

My tentacles tighten their grip on Alex's ankles. Alex's determined glare is irritating. I want to wipe that smug look off her face and replace it with one of pleasure. Does she know what she's doing to me?

"You don't mean that," I respond, my voice dipping low.

Alex squares her shoulders. "What makes you think I don't?"

"The way you reacted after the last time I fucked you."

She shrugs. "I can change my mind."

I let out a groan. This new, teasing side to Alex is giving me major whiplash. When did she become so flirty? I like it —a lot. But I can't give in until I'm sure she wants this.

Alex quirks an eyebrow. "Unless you've changed your mind."

"No!" I growl. "I would never change my mind about you."

"So, what are you waiting for?"

My tentacles itch to slide up her legs, but I keep them at bay. "I need your consent."

"You don't take me asking you to fuck me as consent?"

I lean in close, my breath against her cheek. "I need you to agree to all of it. We're on a boat, Alex. You can't run away from me if you regret this."

Alex shivers. "I agree to everything. I won't regret this."

Even if it's just for tonight, I want her. No, I *need* her.

I smile. All manner of wicked thoughts flow through my mind. "What are we going to do about that smart mouth of yours, my grumpy girl?"

"Why? Are you going to spank me or something?" A defiant giggle bubbles from her lips.

"Do you want to be spanked?"

Alex's eyebrows wiggle. "Maybe."

I step away, my tentacles releasing their grip.

"Where are you going?" The shock on her face would be comical if I weren't so turned on.

"Turn off the stove. We don't want to ruin dinner."

Alex reaches behind her and flicks off the burner. "Now what?"

I chuckle. "You're so impatient tonight. If you want to be fucked properly, you need to undress."

She hurries to take off her shirt, fumbling with the buttons. My breath hitches. I saw Alex naked last night, but I didn't get the chance to admire her. Instead, I was too busy suffering from the lack of water. My heart races faster with each item of clothing she removes.

When Alex is finally bare before me, I suck in a reverent breath. Sucker-shaped hickeys dot her breasts from the other night. My chest swells with pride. She looks damn sexy, covered in my love marks. Adding to her allure are her thick thighs, large and luscious breasts, and soft tummy. I can't wait to see how my tentacles look wrapped around her naked body.

"Is this okay?" Alex asks. Her voice has a slight quiver. She's nervous.

"You're beautiful, Alex."

Her cheeks flush an intriguing pink. I look forward to making them as red as they can get.

I nod towards the corner of the cabin. "Get on the bed."

Alex bites back a smile as she makes her way to the bed. I love the view of her lush hips and ass swaying. The clothes Alex usually wears hide her figure. Seeing it on display is a special treat just for me, and I intend to enjoy her body thoroughly.

Just as Alex is about to sit on the bed, I stop her. "I want you on your hands and knees."

Her eyes widen before narrowing. "You're being awfully bossy."

I approach the bed, drawing myself taller. "I told you I would do something about your mouth."

Alex lets out a small squeak when I wrap her in my tentacles, suspending her so her face is an inch from mine. Cupping her chin in my hand, I bring my lips to hers in a soft kiss. She breathes into my kiss, opening her mouth so I can sweep my tongue over hers. Our kiss is tender, like my feelings for her.

But once the smell of her arousal tickles my nose, I nip at her lower lip. "I'm going to fuck you now, Alex. I need you to communicate if you no longer consent. I take 'no' seriously. Do you understand?"

She nods. "I understand."

I give her one last lingering kiss before lowering her to the bed. "On your hands and knees."

Alex scrambles to obey. I slide onto the bed, settling behind her. My tentacles writhe, reaching for her, but I keep them under control and admire the delectable view of her eager ass in the air. Her cunt is already glistening with her arousal. One of my biggest regrets of the first night I fucked her is that I never got to taste her. I'm not letting that opportunity pass again.

I dip a knuckle into her entrance, careful not to use my claws. Alex quivers at my touch. When I bring my finger to my mouth, I let out a groan as I lick her arousal. She's delicious. What's the best way to get more from her? I lay on my back, positioning myself so my face is between her thighs, and I have a glorious view of her dripping cunt.

"What are you doing?" Alex sits up, but I wrap two tentacles around each ankle, anchoring her to the bed.

"Lower yourself onto my face."

"Maris, I might hurt you." Her voice rises an octave.

I grab a thigh in each hand. "I'm an ancient kraken. Do you think I'm weak?"

"N-no."

"Then sit on my face and let me taste that cunt of yours." I pull her towards me until she's comfortably seated on me. The view is spectacular as I can see her breasts heave and her flushed face.

Alex lets out a moan when I drag my tongue from core to clit. As much as I love her taste, I must pay attention to the sensitive bundle of nerves if I want her to come. I focus my attention there, flattening my tongue so I can lap at her clit. Her legs quake in pleasure, and she falls forward onto her hands, unable to stay upright.

This position blocks my ability to see her reaction to my ministrations. I reach up with my tentacles and clasp Alex's hands behind her back, forcing her to sit upright. One of my tentacles binds her hands while another wraps around her waist to support her.

I continue to lick and suck at her clit, occasionally dipping my tongue into her hot cunt to get a taste. Alex rocks against my face, silently begging for more. My lips become wetter as she gets closer to the edge. I want to taste her as she comes. The tentacle around her waist stretches to her clit and latches on, allowing me to shove my tongue inside her.

"Maris! Oh fuck!" Alex cries as she begins to bounce on my face.

Her cunt flutters around my tongue, and a gush of arousal coats my mouth. I don't cease the onslaught on her clit by my tentacle. Alex writhes, but my tentacles keep her from unseating herself from my face. I need more. She's too delicious to stop.

"Maris! It's too much!" She shrieks in pleasure as her entire body quivers.

With one last hard suck and a lap of my tongue, I release her. Alex falls forward, breathing heavily. I give her clit a soft kiss, and she shivers at the sensation.

"Fuck, Maris. I'm too sensitive now."

I chuckle and slide out from under her. "I'm not done with you yet, my grumpy girl."

Alex groans. "But I finished."

I pepper her ass and hips with kisses. "Who says you can't come more than once?"

"Oh, god."

"Are you praying?" I ask with a smirk.

She pants. "When I come that hard, how could I not?"

A tentacle stretches forward, gripping her chin. "What are you praying for, Alex?"

"To fuck me until I come again."

"That's my good grumpy girl," I praise with a grin.

I turn her around and snatch her hands behind her back

again, securely wrapping a tentacle around her wrists. Alex cries out as I suction another to her hardened nipples, but it comes out strangled as I wrap one around her neck at the same time.

"Is this okay?" I ask.

"Stop asking me if I'm okay and just fuck me already," she whines.

I tut. "That attitude simply won't do. I know just the way to put a stop to that smart mouth."

The tentacle gripping her chin prods her lips. Alex obliges and opens her mouth, allowing me entrance. Pleasure zings to my core when she strokes her tongue over my sensitive suckers. I let out a throaty moan and slide deeper.

My breathing is heavy as I attempt to control myself. "If at any point you want me to remove my tentacle, just give me a little bite. Nod your head if you understand."

Alex looks back at me, her eyes glinting with glee, and nods. Seeing her pouty lips stretched around my tentacle unlocks something feral in me. I shove my tentacle deeper, causing her to gag. I manage to pause, but barely. Did I go too far? Instead of revolting against the intrusion, she hollows her cheeks and sucks.

"Alex!" I moan. A ferocious need to have all of her takes over.

I slip a tentacle into Alex's soaked cunt. She lets out a muffled groan and wiggles her hips, begging for more. I adjust my tentacle so it can also suck her clit. But it's not enough. I need more.

After swiping another tentacle through her arousal, I gently poke at the entrance to her ass. Even through my red-hazed lust, I know I need to be careful. Thomas taught me that much. A deep guttural sound emits from Alex and grinds into my tentacles.

"Do you want to be filled to the brim, my darling grumpy girl?" I purr.

Alex nods furiously, rocking her hips into me. I slip more of my tentacle into her ass, stretching her slowly. When I go as deep as I feel comfortable, I stop and admire the pretty picture I've made for myself.

A tentacle fills every one of her holes while another binds her hands behind her back. The tentacle across her breasts squeezes as it sucks, as does the one around her neck. Fuck, does it feel good to have all my tentacles occupied in Alex's pleasure. I dig one hand into her hip's soft, generous flesh, and tangle the other into her silky tresses, keeping her head turned to the side so I can see her face.

"You're so beautiful," I pant, admiring her while trying to maintain my composure. "I can't believe I get to fuck such a pretty human."

I thrust in and out of her cunt, ass, and mouth, savoring how hot, tight, and wet she feels. Alex moves with me, contracting and sucking around me. Tears well in her eyes, but not with pain or sadness. Instead, they shine with overwhelming pleasure. My mate is about to reach her climax. I push deeper inside where I can, increasing the tempo.

"That's it, my good girl. You're not so grumpy now that you're about to come."

Alex emits a low whine, the mild vibration tickling my already stimulated suckers. I increase the tempo of my thrusts, hoping to take her over the edge with me. With a muffled scream, Alex's pleasure peaks. I crest as her cunt and ass contracts around my swollen tentacles. Everything melts away other than her wet warmth. I'm lost in the sensation of her.

As I come down from my orgasm, my tentacles shrink to their normal size. But I'm still careful as I slide out of Alex. I don't want to hurt her. With a collective gasp, we collapse on the bed in an exhausted heap.

I prop myself on my elbow so I can admire Alex's flushed skin and heaving breasts. Her eyes still shine with the tears she shed while coming. How was I so fortunate to have such an alluring mate?

"What?" Alex pants, a soft smile on her lips.

"I meant what I said."

"When?"

"Earlier." I run my fingers through her hair. "You're beautiful. I don't know what I did to be lucky enough to have you, even if just for tonight."

Alex rolls onto her side to face me better. "Maris, about tonight—"

I cringe. Here it comes—her regret.

She takes my hand in hers. "I don't want it to be just for tonight."

My eyes widen. Could it be? Could Alex want to be my mate?

I open my mouth to ask for clarification when the boat rocks. The roar of water is deafening, even from inside the cabin.

"Maris!" A deep, guttural voice roars. "I know you're in there."

I gasp. It's my father.

Chapter 14
Alex

"Caspian?" I grip the bed for leverage as the boat continues to rock. "He's here?"

Maris wraps a tentacle around me to keep me from flying across the cabin. "Sounds like it. We better get out there before he gets mad."

"How did he find us?"

"I bet he sensed my magic during my soak. He's a very powerful kraken." Maris scoops the quilt off the bed and drapes it around me.

I admire her handiwork. She's turned the quilt into some sort of wrap dress. I would rather be in my real clothes, but I don't have a choice if we're in a rush.

Maris keeps a tentacle around my waist as we stumble onto the deck. By 'we,' I mean 'me.' Maris, on the other hand, glides out of the cabin with ease. I would hate her right now if she hadn't just fucked me into jelly.

What's waiting for us in the ocean when we step onto the deck takes my breath away, but not in a good way. I'm too terrified to breathe. Before us is a wall of textured flesh;

it's too dark to make out the color, but I would guess a deep gray in the moonlight.

I crane my neck to see how high the skin barrier blocking my view of the ocean goes. I wish I hadn't. It towers over us like a massive cruise ship. Sitting atop this fleshy wall are two large golden eyes that shine in the dark. If that isn't horrifying enough, an immense mouth full of dagger-like teeth looms over a squirming mass of tentacles. My knees would have buckled beneath me if it weren't for Maris holding me by the waist.

"Father!" Maris laughs in delight as if a colossal monster isn't gnashing his teeth a mere few feet away.

"My daughter!" booms the creature. He angles his head to get a better look at me. "And a little human!"

Being in his gaze makes my blood run cold. The shivers that ran through me when I saw the mermaid are nothing compared to the terror I feel now. I open my mouth to scream, but Maris slaps a hand over it, muffling my shriek of terror.

"Don't scream," she murmurs under her breath. "My father won't hurt you if you don't act like prey."

When she drops her hand, I ask, "Is that thing really your father?"

"Yes. I didn't think he would appear like this. My apologies. I should have warned you that this was a possibility."

I stare at her, slack-jawed. "No shit, Maris. I'm on the verge of freaking out."

A loud rumbling sound comes from Caspian that must be a laugh. "Little human, do not be afraid. You have Maris's scent. You must be her mate."

Her scent? I look to Maris for an explanation, but a devilish smile glints at me in the moonlight.

"This is Alex," she proudly proclaims, wrapping another tentacle around me.

That's fine with me. I feel safe in her embrace, and she's holding me too tight for me to run and hide. Not that hiding would do me any good. Caspian could destroy Bryan's boat with a whack from one of his many tentacles.

"Nice to meet you, little Alex. I hope you make my daughter happy." Caspian's voice has a hint of warmth.

There's silence between us. Maris eyes me. *Oh. She must expect me to respond.*

"Uh…" My voice comes out as a squeak. I clear my throat and try again. "Nice to meet you too, Caspian."

He peers at me a moment longer as if sizing me up. When he finally turns his attention to Maris, I discreetly blow out a sigh of relief.

"Maris, my daughter. Where have you been? I came to visit, but you were gone. The creatures in your den said you had been abducted. I tried to follow your scent, but it disappeared. I feared the worst. I'm relieved you're alive. And you come back with a mate! How delightful!"

Abducted? By who? And how did she end up in my pool if she was kidnapped? I look at Maris, expecting her to be just as confused as me, but instead, she's an ashy white. Literally, her skin changed color, like an octopus. Her gaze is far away and glassy. *Oh shit. She's in shock.* Maris must be remembering what happened to her.

"Maris?" I place a hand on her cheek, urging her to return to me.

She doesn't respond. Maris's grip on me becomes slack.

"What is wrong with my daughter?" Caspian roars.

I quake, terrified of his anger, and collapse because I'm no longer safely in Maris's grasp.

A guttural growl emits from Caspian. "Answer me, coward!"

If Caspian doesn't calm down, he will destroy this boat and me. I get it. His daughter went missing, and now she's catatonic. I would be losing my cool, too.

"Her memories!" I force myself to stand despite my trembling legs. "She's lost them."

"What do you mean?"

"I found Maris at the bottom of my pool." I rush to answer. "When she woke up, she had no memories. We've slowly recovered most of them, but we still don't know how she ended up in my pool. I'm guessing something you said triggered her to remember."

Caspian scoops up Maris with one of his giant tentacles. I have to jump out of the way to avoid him knocking me over.

"What are you doing?" I shriek.

He ignores me, bringing Maris to eye level. "If you do not come to, Maris, I will take your pretty mate with me beneath the waves."

I gulp back a whimper. Maris said not to act like prey, but every fiber of my being is screaming for me to get the fuck out of here. Which is stupid because we're in the middle of the ocean. There's nowhere to go. Hopefully, it's an empty threat to jar Maris awake, but it doesn't stop it from being any less terrifying.

"You wouldn't dare," Maris bellows.

It's difficult to see what's going on above me with how dark it is, but I can barely make out Maris squirming in her father's grasp before a black stream of fluid hits him in the eye. *Oh shit.* Did she just squirt a liquid at him? My guess is ink. This isn't good. If she hurt him, he might retaliate by killing us both.

Instead, Caspian roars with thunderous laughter. "I am pleased my daughter would fight fiercely for her mate." He lowers Maris back to the boat. "You could have transformed if you wanted to be a real threat."

When Maris's tentacle touches the boat deck, she pulls me against her. "Did he hurt you?" she asks, checking me for injuries.

"No, not at all," I reassure her. "What does he mean by 'transform?'"

She doesn't answer me, pulling me in for a kiss instead. It's a deep kiss, tasting of relief and appreciation. Her eyes shine with tears when she pulls away, and she's back to her usual shades of blue and seafoam.

"Promise me something?" Maris strokes my cheek with her claw.

"Anything."

"You'll look away if I ever have to take on my colossal form."

My jaw drops. Maris can turn into an enormous nightmare as well? My stomach twists. She never told me this.

"I—" What do I even say? Seeing Maris as a giant monster sounds both terrifying and intriguing. Would she have a massive maw of teeth as well? Would she still be beautiful?

"Promise me, Alex," she demands.

Her teeth clamp down on her lower lip, fangs digging into the plush flesh. She'll draw blood if she's not careful.

I lean in and press my lips to her in a gentle kiss. "I promise I won't look."

Maris sighs into my mouth. "Thank you," she murmurs against my lips.

The boat sways as Caspian lowers himself so he doesn't

tower as high over us. "Do you remember what happened, Maris?"

"I do." She nods. "My companions are correct. I was abducted."

"What?" Caspian and I both exclaim.

Caspian quakes, his golden eyes flashing. "Who do I need to rip to shreds?"

"They were two human fishermen."

"But you disappeared?" I interject. "The mermaid said you never resurfaced."

"It was partially correct." Maris turns to Caspian. "Keep me honest, but after Thomas died, I slipped into a depression and rarely left my dwelling. The only visitors I had were my creature companions and my father. But I've felt more like myself over the past few moons."

Caspian's tentacles quiver. "That's correct. You'd been resurfacing occasionally to watch the sunrise, your favorite time of the day."

"I'm careful not to resurface near boats, and I dive back down as soon as the sky is blue. But this time, I got a little carried away by the sight. The clouds were extra fluffy that morning. I didn't hear the quiet fishing boat approach until it was too late..."

Chapter 15
Maris

"That one looks like a cat," I murmured to no one, pointing to the sky.

The large white cloud resembled Mister Tibs. I smiled softly realizing that it wasn't quite so painful thinking about my friends anymore. The guilt was easing. Even though the Royal Navy had captured a few of them, most of them had escaped and were still alive, including Thomas's lover and first mate. I just wished I'd at least resurfaced to see them again.

A small splash startled me from my reminiscence. I snapped my head to face two humans holding a net on the edge of a mid-sized fishing boat a few fathoms away. I rolled my eyes, thinking them fools. Slipping below the surface and avoiding their net would be too easy. The best part was that no one would believe them when they told their bizarre tale of some unknown creature in the ocean. Why are they even attempting to capture me?

I offered them a small wave and a crooked smile before diving under the water. But something wasn't right. A flash *of light blinded me, and a loud bang pierced my ears right before I blacked out.*

When I came to, my head was pounding. Even the sound of waves lapping against the boat was like someone taking a hammer to my temple. Boat? I was on a boat? Fuck. I tried to move, but my body felt heavy and tangled in itself.

Regretfully, I opened my eyes and winced against the bright sun. But I instantly recognized the chunks of thick rope that blocked my view of the sky. I was in a fisherman's net.

"Joey!" A voice I didn't recognize shouted from above me. "It's moving."

I focused my vision on the voice. One of the fishermen loomed over me, close enough for me to snatch that crusty gray beard of his, and I would have, but I still couldn't move that much.

The second fisherman popped into view. "Don't get so close to it, Frank!"

Frank rolled his eyes. "The damn thing is still stunned. We'll just give it a good whack over the head and put it right back to sleep."

"Are you sure this is a good idea?" Joey asked, scratching his head through his bright red baseball cap.

"Yes, Joey!" Frank snapped. "How many times do I have to tell you? I know a guy."

"And this guy is gonna pay us for this thing?"

Frank stood, shoving Joey. "I've already told you. The

answer is 'yes.' And I'll deck the shit out of you if you ask again. No more questions. Give this thing a good hit, but be careful not to kill it. We're lucky the dynamite didn't."

Dynamite fishers. I hadn't encountered one, but my father had told me about these human pests. I tried again to move, but my limbs were too heavy. All I could do was weakly contract my tentacles, and it hurt so bad I nearly screamed. But it was nothing compared to the blow Joey gave my head with a wooden paddle. I saw stars before my world went pitch dark.

I was being dragged. Each scrape of my skin against the deck was agony. How long had they kept me out of the water? But I clamped my eyes and mouth shut and my body still. I didn't want the fishermen to know I was awake.

"This fucking thing is so heavy, man," Joe whined.

Frank grunted. "Kindly shut the fuck up. We just gotta get this thing to our truck; then we'll be rich men."

"Not until we deliver it to the airfield and your guy hands us the cash." Joey panted, clearly struggling with my weight.

"Whatever. Just keep pulling."

I wiggled a finger, testing my mobility. It hurt, but it was easier than before. Thomas taught me that patience was the most important virtue. I needed to remember that right now. If I moved too soon, I might not have enough strength to escape before they hit me again. If I waited too long, I risked these idiots handing me off to someone more competent.

Monster hunters had been around since before I'd been born. Some humans wished to keep us monsters as pets, but most wanted just to harvest our organs for their magical properties. Unless humans had figured out a way to keep us from transforming into our monstrous form to keep me in a cage, I was going to be murdered for my heart, which could extend the lives of mortals.

So, I waited as they moved me. My heart rate spiked when I was no longer on the boat. This was my first time on dry land. I hated that I couldn't feel the tide anymore. Us krakens were tied to the moon's push and pull, and we couldn't feel her when we weren't in the ocean. At least on a boat, the gentle rock of the waves kept me connected.

With a strained heave, they lifted me into their 'truck' with no care or attempt to be gentle. It took everything in me not to let out a pained whimper.

"How are we gonna keep people from seeing it?" Joey asked, out of breath.

Frank scoffed. "You act like your big cousin Frank hasn't thought of everything. We'll just use the tarp. Go get it!"

"Why do I gotta get it?"

"Because someone's gotta guard this thing. Now get to it before I whoop your ass."

Joey whimpered, but his footsteps faded away. A few moments later, the sunlight dimmed, and a heavy crinkling sheet settled around me. I cautiously opened my eyes to darkness. This tarp must have blocked out the sun.

I listened closely to the fishermen as they argued which route to take to the airfield. Frank won by bullying Joey into submission, who whined in defeat. I couldn't wait to get away from these assholes. They were really freaking annoying.

A roar and rumble startled me, but I was still too weak to move. The truck lurched forward, and we were on the move. It had to be some kind of boat for on the land. I was careful with my movements, testing my motor skills but hopefully not drawing any attention to myself. I couldn't hear the kidnappers over the noises of the truck.

We occasionally came to a stop, and when we did, a frightening cacophony of other noises assaulted my ears. Through the sounds of people chattering, loud horns, and other landboats, I could still hear the squawking of seagulls.

That's promising. That meant we were still close to the ocean. I began to wiggle my way from underneath the net. Thankfully, my mobility had come back enough for me to make quick work of it, especially with my tentacles.

When we came to a stop, and the only sound was the rumbling of the truck, I knew I had my chance. It meant no one else was around. I willed myself to transform into a human. A human woman would attract less attention than a kraken.

With a burst of energy, I sat up, making my world spin as a white-hot pain jolted behind my eyes. But I didn't have time for my headache to ease. I threw the tarp off me, the sunlight searing into my throbbing head. With unsteady legs, I heaved myself out of the truck.

"Hey! What the fuck? Is that a naked lady?" Frank shouted.

I didn't look back. The fishermen didn't realize I was the creature they'd captured. Yet. I broke into a wobbly run. It'd been a long time since I'd used my human legs, so the sprint was more of a fast stumble, but it still got me away from the truck. Besides my pounding head, the ground was burning my feet. Why is it so hot?

The scent of the sea was faint, which was a problem because I needed water. I looked around as I ran. The glint of sunlight off the water caught my eye. It wasn't the ocean, but it would have to do.

Fuck. *An iron railing spanned the perimeter of the water. Did I have the strength to scale it? It didn't matter. I needed in there. Fast. Thankfully, the railing was only about a fathom high, so hoisting myself over it wasn't as tricky as it could have been. But that didn't stop the endeavor from being any less exhausting.*

I landed on my hands and knees, panting from fatigue, the pain in my head blurring my vision. On top of it all, my skin felt like it was fire. Slowly, I crawled towards the water, digging my human nails into the rough, hot ground.

Through the grace of the goddess, I made it to the water. With a deep sigh, I leaned forward and fell headfirst into the water, transforming into a kraken as soon as I splashed the surface. The rush of cool liquid instantly soothed my burning skin. But something wasn't right. The water felt weird. It wasn't salt, but it wasn't the fresh kind that Thomas and the other sailors drank. It tasted bitter, and I almost vomited.

My vision swam. Shit. *I was losing consciousness. I didn't know if it was the head trauma, the strange water, or a combination of both, but I couldn't focus anymore. What if the fishermen realized I was gone? Would they recognize the naked woman they saw running was me? I needed to remain awake.*

But what if I took a small nap? Krakens heal after rest in the water. Yeah. That's what I need—just a little sleep.

The next thing I knew, I was staring at the face of an angel. She was the most beautiful thing I'd ever seen. My heart fluttered. This woman was something special to me. I'd waited my whole life to find my mate. Could she be mine?

I grabbed the angel's wrist. She needed to know I was in danger. Maybe she would help me.

"You're alive!" she cried.

"Don't let them take my heart," I wheezed. I couldn't let my heart fall into the wrong hands. If hunters got ahold of me, I would give some terrible person a longer life.

"Who? And what are they taking?"

But her voice was distant. I couldn't hold on anymore. I focused on her face before darkness took over once more.

Chapter 16
Alex

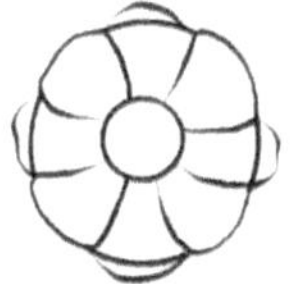

Caspian and I are quiet, absorbing Maris's recollection of what happened. I've never been more angry in my life. Two assholes hurt Maris and had every intention of trafficking her to someone who planned on harvesting her heart.

"When I find out who Joey and Frank are, I will beat the shit of them myself," I growl.

Caspian chuckles, the sound low and deep. "You're a feisty human. I like you."

I would beam under his praises if I weren't still steaming over Maris's story.

Maris's eyes glaze over, and her mouth falls open in shock. "I don't think our biggest concern is the fishermen."

I quirk an eyebrow. "What do you mean?"

"It's whoever they were going to pass me off to. There's a chance that person is a professional monster hunter."

I take her hand in mine, attempting to comfort her. "How would they know where you went? You're safe now."

She grimaces.

"What?"

Caspian sighs, his breath ruffling my hair. "Professional monster hunters are resourceful. They likely already know where Maris has been dwelling and who has been helping her."

Oh. That's not good. The hunters probably know where I live. They might even know about me, too.

Shit...what about Ella and Avery? They've been helping us! "We have to go home." I grab Maris by the shoulders. "Now."

She nods, then turns to Caspian. "Thank you for your help, Father."

He touches Maris with one of his massive tentacles. "Do you need my assistance?"

Maris shakes her head. "I know how hard it is for you to maintain human glamor at your size. I don't want to risk anything happening to you. I appreciate the offer."

"Understood. Go confront the hunters. But promise me you'll visit. I've missed you, daughter. This is the happiest I've ever seen you."

Maris pops a kiss on Caspian's tentacle. "I promise."

The moment is precious. I don't want to rush it along, but every minute we aren't back on Sunshine Key is a minute that Ella and Avery are potentially in danger. Thankfully, Maris's moment with her father passes quickly. Caspian returns below the surface, making minimal waves as he sinks.

My stomach drops when I see Maris's face. Her mouth forms a pinched line, and her brows knit together. Does she regret not going with her father?

I place a hand on her shoulder. "Are you okay?"

She turns to me with a ghost of a smile. "I'm sorry that I've put everyone in danger."

My sweet Maris is always so concerned for everyone else. I take her face in my hands, standing on my tiptoes to bring her mouth towards mine in a gentle kiss. She sighs, pulling me close. I sink into her, deepening the kiss.

I need Maris to know that I don't blame her, that I'm happy she came into my life, and that she has nothing to be sorry for. There are so many things I want and need to tell her, but now is not the time. I pour all these unspoken sentiments into our kiss, hoping she hears me.

"Don't apologize," I murmur against her mouth. "You can't blame yourself for this."

Maris runs her claws through my hair. "Thank you, Alex. You are too good to me."

I press a quick kiss to her nose. "It's natural with you."

We don't bother going back to Miami first, instead setting course for Sunshine Key. I am sure Bryan will understand. Besides, we'll return the boat as soon as we discover Avery and Ella safe.

Maris gives me plenty of breathing room to focus on navigating. I appreciate her quiet support as my mind dashes with thoughts of Avery and Ella. What if the monster hunters found them? Avery will fight back until her dying breath, and Ella is stronger than she lets on; I want to believe they can handle themselves. But if these people are professionals, I don't know what they might be capable of.

As soon as we have cell service, I ask Maris to take

control of the boat so I can call Bryan. I need to let him know we are taking the boat directly to Sunshine Key.

He answers the phone on the first ring. "Alex? Have you heard from Ella?" he asks in a panic. "She hasn't been answering her phone. Wait. How are you calling? I thought you would be out of cell range until later today."

"Uh...well...I had a bad feeling," I lie, hating the way it tastes on my tongue. I can't tell Bryan about krakens and monster hunters. He's already freaking out about Ella; I can't add to his already fraying nerves.

"A bad feeling? About Ella?"

"I'm not sure." It's not a lie. I can't know for certain how I feel until we find out if the monster hunters are after her. "Tell me what's going on with Ella."

"We have weekly video chats to catch up, but she never called last night. When I tried calling her, she never answered, and she still hasn't."

My stomach sinks. That isn't like Ella. She's reliable. She wouldn't ignore her dad. "Have you tried Avery? Maybe she can go check on her."

"That's a great idea, Alex. I'll hang up and call Avery."

"Before you go, uh, we aren't on our way back to Miami. We're sailing to Sunshine Key."

There's a long silence on the other end. I think we've lost connection but he finally responds. "What?"

"I'm sorry! We'll bring it back as soon as are sure Ella is safe."

"Is there something you're not telling me?" he asks, donning his fatherly voice.

Fuck. "I think I'm losing service."

"That's bullshit, Alex. If you don't tell me what's going on, I'm coming down—"

I hang up on him before he can finish his sentence.

We'll make it to Sunshine Key before he does, hopefully ensuring Ella's safety before we have to get Bryan involved.

I head back to the helm and tell Maris about Ella.

"Maybe she's busy?" she suggests, stepping aside so I can take over the controls.

"That's not like Ella."

She doesn't respond, instead wrapping me in a tight embrace. I allow myself a few deep breaths to calm down. Maris's familiar scent of ocean breeze and citrus soothes my racing heart. As long we're together, we'll get through this.

When I feel ready to refocus, I give Maris a quick kiss on the cheek. "Thank you."

"Anything for you."

Thankfully, the marina isn't busy, so docking is quick and painless. By the time we dock, I have dozens of texts, several missed calls, and a voicemail from Bryan. I don't even bother listening. I need an instant update, so I call him back, putting him on speaker so Maris can be up to date as well.

"Any word?" I ask, as soon as he answers.

"None. And Avery isn't answering her phone either. I tried to call the police, but they can't do anything about someone not answering my calls."

"Shit," I mutter.

Maris places a comforting hand on my shoulder. "They'll be okay."

"Alex," Bryan shouts. "What is going on? I'm trying to

book a flight down there, but I'm having no luck. I'm freaking the fuck out."

My throat bobs. "We just docked, and tracking down Ella is our first priority."

"I'm driving down there. Fuck the airport."

I glance back at Maris, who looks at me wide-eyed. Without even speaking, I know we share the same sentiment—we don't want to endanger another person.

"I know you're worried about Ella. I am, too. But let's think logically here. How likely is it that anything happened to her? She probably just lost her phone."

"Then why are you back at Sunshine Key and not enjoying a romantic getaway with your new girlfriend?"

"Maybe the bad feeling isn't even about Ella, or maybe I'm just paranoid. But, Bryan, traffic on the Overseas Highway is insane. I bet we'll find her within the next hour. Besides, can you afford to leave work at the last minute?"

Bryan is a dive instructor. He has classes on specific days of the week, and I know tomorrow is one of those days.

"I will cancel for my daughter," he says. No-nonsense Bryan is scary.

"Let me try to get in touch with Ella first," I say, attempting to sound as confident and calm as possible, even though I'm forcing myself not to freak out. "Besides, I bet Avery will call back any minute, knowing exactly where Ella is."

Once again, the line is silent. Bryan is a determined man who loves his daughter very much. I won't be surprised if he chooses to ignore my request. And I wouldn't even be mad about it. I get it. This is Ella and Avery we're talking about.

A long sigh hisses through his teeth. "Fine. I don't like it, but you're right. We need to exhaust every resource first."

I close my eyes, saying a silent thank you to whoever is watching over us that we aren't also putting Byran in harm's way.

"We just finished anchoring. I'm going to hail us a cab, and I'll call within the next hour with updates."

"If I don't hear from you, I'm heading down there."

There's no arguing with him on this. His tone was too firm, too final. "Deal. Talk to you soon."

When I hang up, Maris and I exchange nervous glances. We don't grab anything off the boat, not even our duffel bag.

"We'll head to my house, grab my moped, then drive around looking for Ella," I explain to Maris.

She nods. "Where will we look first?"

"We'll stop by Avery's first since it's the closest to my place."

As we race towards the marina entrance, we pass locals and tourists alike, enjoying the lovely weather. It's jarring, seeing people go on with their lives while I'm having a crisis. No one knows I'm in the company of a kraken disguised as a beautiful woman and rushing back to Sunshine Key to find out if monster hunters kidnapped my best friend and sister.

Thankfully, an empty cab is idling at the marina entrance, awaiting boating tourists who may need transportation. In hushed whispers on the short ride back to my house, we list everywhere we'll look before declaring Ella and Avery missing. There's a little relief that we have a plan, but it's upsetting that no one has heard from Ella in almost 24 hours, and I haven't spoken to Avery since the morning we left for Miami. The sinking feeling in my gut tells me the monster hunters have something to do with this.

The cab pulls into my driveway, and I shove a wad of cash in the driver's hand. He doesn't even have a chance to park before I scramble out of the back seat. There's no time to waste.

"Bye! Thank you!" Maris calls back to the cab driver as we bound up the stairs.

My heart leaps in my throat when I reach my door. It's slightly ajar. I know I locked it before I left. Have the hunters been here? There's only one way to find out. I suck in a breath and lift my hand to push open the door.

"Alex, wait!" Maris reaches for my arm, but it's too late.

The door swings open, revealing Avery and Ella bound to kitchen chairs by their wrists and ankles. Their mouths have been stuffed with black cloth, but their muffled screams still make their way through the makeshift gags.

Maris wraps her arms around my waist in an attempt to stop me from rushing towards them. I throw all my weight forward, forcing her to stumble and let me go. The monster hunters must have left them here. I don't know if they'll be back, but I can't risk it; I need to untie Avery and Ella now.

"Alex!" Maris shrieks.

But I don't stop. I reach for my sister and best friend. They're safe now that Maris and I here. We'll get them out of this horrible situation.

A mechanical click stops me. My blood runs cold. Someone in my house has a gun.

The hard press of metal against the back of my head makes me sick. I swallow back bile.

"Don't move," a man's nasally voice growls.

Shit. It must be monster hunters.

A soft puff of air followed by a heavy thud causes me to flinch. Ella and Avery scream behind their gags. Tears stream down Ella's cheeks, while Avery looks murderous.

"I said not to move. Do it again, and I'll shoot your friends."

A second, deeper voice chimes in. "It's down. That tranq worked fast."

"Don't hesitate," the owner of the first voice snaps. "Tie it up before it wakes."

It? But before I can process what they might be talking about, I hiss in pain. The man behind me fists my hair at the scalp, jerking me around to face him. A long, angular face with slicked greasy black hair stares at me as if bored.

"The kraken aimed to protect you. Why?"

My eyes fall to a pile of limbs on the floor behind him. Maris. That loud thump must have been her. They tranquilized her, and now she's back in her kraken form. The second man, who must be almost seven feet tall and as wide as my doorway, roughly bounds her wrists and tentacles.

The man with black hair licks his teeth. "And I can see you care about her. What is your relationship to her?"

I clamp my teeth together. There's no way this piece of shit is getting any information from me.

"Oh. So you don't want to talk?" He sneers. "That's alright." He snaps his fingers. "Georgie, why don't you show this young lady what happens when she doesn't cooperate."

With one last tug on Maris's restraints, the big hunter rises. "Yes, Sergeant." He stalks toward Avery and Ella.

"Wait!" I cry when Georgie pulls out a switchblade. I can't let him hurt my best friend and sister.

A sinister grin reveals Sergeant's too-small teeth. "Do you have something to say now?"

"I'm her mate," I admit through gritted teeth. I hate myself for revealing this to these assholes, but if I let them hurt Avery or Ella, I would never forgive myself.

"Mate?" Georgie asks this question as if he's never heard the term before.

"Perfect." Sergeant snickers. "You may prove to be useful."

"Uh...should we be messing with a kraken's mate?"

"What better way to control it than with the thing it values most." Sergeant rolls his eyes as if Georgie just asked the dumbest thing in the world.

But Georgie has a point. I've seen Maris be protective of me, and it's scary—not for me, but for those threatening me.

Georgie lets out a nervous chuckle. Good. He should be worried. "I guess you're right."

"Of course, I'm right," his companion snaps. "Search the mate for anything of value. Leave her cell phone here. We're taking her with us, and I don't want anyone tracking her."

The oversized man paws at my pocket, fishing out my cell phone, keys, and utility knife. George deposits the items onto my side table.

Sergeant finally lowers the gun, leaning in close enough for me to smell his putrid breath. I don't cringe away. I won't let him see how terrified I am.

"Here's the deal," he hisses. "We're going to walk out of this shit hole together, peacefully, like we're old friends. I don't want any of the neighbors getting suspicious. An associate is waiting down the street, ready to pick us up. You're going to get in without a struggle. If you so much as fart wrong, I'll put a bullet through your head, and I'll send

Georgie back in to show your friends just how much you care for their wellbeing. Understand?"

I hate this piece of shit. I fight the urge to spit in his face; that wouldn't do anyone any good. "Understood," I say through gritted teeth.

Sergeant pats my face with his hand. "Smart girl." He snaps his beady eyes to Georgie. "Roll the kraken in the carpet."

"What about my friends?" I cry.

Sergeant narrows his eyes at me.

I square my shoulders. I'm not going to let this asshole intimidate me. "They have nothing to do with this."

"You think I'm going to let them go? No, ma'am. Too risky."

What? No! He wouldn't hurt them. I'm doing everything he said. Tears blur my vision, but I swallow them back. I won't let them see my cry.

Sergeant quirks his eyebrow. "Oh. Don't worry, sweetcheeks. I won't kill them. But I am leaving them here, safe and sound."

I control my sigh of relief. At least Avery and Ella are safe. Hopefully, they can figure a way out of their bonds.

Georgie's grunts steal my attention. He's rolling Maris in my designer rug. I officially hate that rug. Why was I insistent on having it? Without it, these two goons couldn't transport Maris out of here.

Who am I kidding? They would have found a way.

"Alright, Sergeant. I'm ready." Georgie hefts the rolled carpet with Maris inside onto his shoulder.

Sergeant nudges me forward with the gun. Avery and Ella look at me, their skin ashen in terror.

"It will be okay," I mouth to them. I puff out my chest

and follow Georgie through the door with Sergeant close behind me.

A large black SUV waits for us at the end of my driveway. A stout man in a ball cap hops out and opens the hatchback. Georgie tosses Maris in the back as if she's a bag of trash. I wince. A hand digs into my shoulder.

"You better smile, bitch," Sergeant murmurs into my ear.

I force a grin. Sergeant prods me to get into the back seat. Georgie climbs in next to me. Great. If Sergeant had sat back here, I might have overpowered him with his slight frame. But Georgie? I don't stand a chance. The stout man heaves himself into the driver's seat. He looks at Sergeant, awaiting direction.

Sergeant clips his seatbelt. "To the industrial pier."

The driver nods and puts the vehicle in gear before stepping on the gas pedal. Once we are out of my neighborhood, he holds out his hand, pinching and rubbing his thumb and forefinger together in the universal sign for money.

"You'll have your cut as soon as we get this thing to our buyer." Sergeant scowls. "And it'll be good, too. No one has caught a kraken in my lifetime. That heart will be worth a fortune."

Georgie shifts in his seat, too large even for this massive SUV. "Remind me again as to why we aren't flying it to the buyer? Won't we get our money faster if we ship by plane?"

The driver snaps his fingers in agreement. I guess this guy doesn't talk.

Sergeant scoffs. "How many times do I have to go over this? Goddamn. Thank fuck the two of you have me to help run this operation. How much more plainly can I word this? Boat equals more control. Plane equals less control. And after the damn thing escaped those idiot fisherman, we need all the control we can get."

Hope surges through me. Sergeant might think he has control over us, but I think we might be able to escape back to Sunshine Key if we're on a boat. Maybe I could even call for Caspian. I'll take any advantage we can get.

"What are we gonna do with her?" Georgie thumbs at me.

"It all depends on whether she's a good girl for us or not." Sergeant turns around to give me a wolfish grin.

I shudder and look out of the window, not wanting to maintain eye contact with the asshole.

"I just think getting a mate involved is messy," Georgie mutters.

"What was that?" Sergeant narrows his eyes at him.

"Nothing," Georgie grumbles.

I wouldn't say I like Georgie, but I hate him less than Sergeant. He still kidnapped my friends and tranquilized Maris. Not to mention the casual way he twirls his switch-blade, cautioning me to behave without verbally threatening me. But still, his advocating for my release is promising. Maybe he can be reasoned with.

Ideally, Maris will wake up at the perfect time for us to escape, then we can go to the police and get these mother fuckers arrested for abduction. Or hopefully, somehow, Ella and Avery are able to free themselves. Maybe they've already called the cops.

I risk turning my head to look in the back. The carpet cocooning Maris isn't moving. She must still be knocked out cold. How long before the tranquilizer wears off? Hopefully soon. The longer she's asleep, the harder it will be to return home.

Chapter 17
Maris

Pain rips through my skull. Why is everything so blurry? And I can't move again. Great. This whole blacking out and being kidnapped thing has really got to stop happening. At least I'm not dead.

Panic grips my chest. Did they hurt Alex? What about Avery and Ella?

Squinting, I look around the room as best as I can. The walls are metal, and wooden crates stacked floor to ceiling fill most of the space. I gasp. Alex is sitting about a fathom away from me, her knees to chest, watching me. We lock eyes. She knows I'm awake but doesn't react as if she knows my strategy.

Her hazel eyes are tired, and her sun-kissed skin is pale and ashen. Dirt cakes her clothing, and her hair is even more disheveled than usual. There's no denying that something is terribly wrong.

I hate that I can't move. Not that I should. If I learned anything from my interaction with the fishermen, it's best they don't know I'm awake until I'm ready.

"She's awake!" exclaims an oily voice.

Ugh. There goes my plan.

A hand belonging to the largest human I've ever seen reaches for Alex and grabs her by the back of her shirt. "I got its mate, Sergeant."

I growl, attempting to sit up, but I'm restrained. On top of lingering heaviness from whatever they shot me with, I'm not going anywhere.

A slender man with an angular face blocks my view of Alex. "I wouldn't move if I were you."

The oily voice must belong to this slender man, Sergeant. He snaps his fingers. "Georgie, show this kraken what happens if it moves."

He steps to the side, allowing me to see the big man holding a blade to Alex's neck. My mate looks at me with pleading eyes. Fury blazes through me, sour and hot. My skin flashes dark red in anger, and my tentacles curl into themselves.

They will rue the day they threatened my mate.

Georgie's eyes widen at my color change. "Uh...let's tranq it again."

"No!" Sergeant snaps. "We've been over this. Too much can damage its tissues. We need it to be as intact as possible. We'll use its mate to control it until we make it to the buyer."

"Touch her and die," I growl.

Sergeant and Georgie look at each other before the former bursts into laughter. I really hate this guy. Georgie, on the other hand, has eyes the size of dinner plates. At least he seems to have some common sense.

"That's a good one," Sergeant sneers. "You make one move, and this blade goes through her neck."

I show my teeth but don't move, unwilling to risk the hunters harming Alex.

Sergeant approaches Alex. "For good measure, so you understand I'm serious." He winds up his arm before backhanding Alex across the face.

I snarl, but my brave mate doesn't give him the satisfaction of any noise. Pride swells in my chest. She is truly a kraken's mate. Alex won't show fear or pain. Instead, she spits blood at his feet.

"You little shit!" Sergeant raises his hand again, and I see red.

This fucker made my mate bleed. My blood boils. I'll sever those filthy hands off his body; then I'll shred them both to pieces before making them a snack for the sharks. Or maybe I'll feed them to mermaids, but not until I rip out their tongues for threatening Alex.

"Uh...Sergeant!" Georgie drops the blade against Alex's neck and begins to back away from her. "I won't hurt her, I promise."

But it's too late. My limbs stretch, and my bones crack and snap as I shift. I'm losing control. It should hurt, but fury numbs all pain.

"I warned you!" My voice booms. "Now you die!"

Chapter 18
Alex

Maris is transforming. The first thing to change is her eyes, morphing from her usual gorgeous gold to empty black. She roars in rage as more tentacles split from her original six. Her head elongates, her features smoothing until she has the head of an octopus. I wince as spines like a lionfish rip through her flesh as her body enlarges.

Her bonds burst apart as she grows, and a giant tentacle wraps tightly around my waist. I cling to the flesh, careful to avoid getting pierced by the spines. Sergeant and Georgie scream as Maris sweeps them up in separate tentacles.

She continues to grow until the ship's walls can't hold her anymore. I screw my eyes shut in terror and cover my head with my arms as the ceiling collapses. But Maris cocoons me in her tentacle, protecting my head from the falling debris.

With a deafening crack, the shipping boat breaks in half, and Maris lands in the ocean with a thunderous splash. I squirm, twisting in her grip to look around me. Debris litters the sea, while a few mariners cling to various wood planks, looking at Maris in horror.

She's massive. Not as large as Caspian, but still terrifying. Her skin's retained her coloring, but now dark blue spines protrude from her body. Thankfully, I don't see any teeth.

My heart sinks. I promised Maris I wouldn't watch if she ever transformed into her colossal form. But it's impossible not to look when she gave no warning. She must have lost control when she saw me hurt.

We escaped, but at what cost? How am I going to calm Maris? I shout her name, and her gaze slides to me. Her giant black eyes are void except for rage. This isn't good. Ear-piercing screams reach my ears. The monster hunters are still tight in her clutches.

"Help!" Sergeant shrieks. He pounds his fist against her tentacle, but I doubt she even feels it.

Maris holds me closer, but the monster hunters howl in pain. I'm going to have to watch my gentle, sweet Maris crush them to death with her tentacles.

To add to this living nightmare, she brings another tentacle to Sergeant, wrapping the tip around Sergeant's wrist. She's going to rip his hands off. I swallow back bile. I won't let Maris kill them, no matter what they planned to do with us. She's never purposefully harmed a human, and I won't allow her to begin now.

"Maris! Stop! Please stop!" I plead.

She looks at me again. Maris doesn't remove her tentacle from Sergeant's wrists, but she's stopped for now.

"Listen to me, Maris." I place a hand on her textured skin, which is rougher than her true form. I miss my velvety Maris. "You don't want to do this."

A rumbling growl is all I get as a response. *Fuck!* Has Maris gone feral?

"Thomas wouldn't want this for you. I don't want this for you."

I gently stroke the tentacle wrapped around me, needing to soothe Maris before she does something she regrets.

"Let them go, Maris." I rest my face against her. "Please? Do it for me."

Maris releases a confusing trill. She must be unsure as to why I would want someone who hurt me to live. That's fine. At least she's thinking past the blind rage.

"One of the things I love most about you is your gentle soul. I love that you would protect me, but I love your capacity for mercy even more."

The tentacle wrapped around Sergeant's wrists drops. But her grip on the monster hunters remains. Being honest with my feelings for her seems to have the effect I want.

"There's so much more I love about you. I love that you listen to me. I love that you take care of me. I love that you're so fun to flirt with, but we can't do any of those things if you stay like this, Maris."

I turn my face so I can press my lips against her skin. "I love your positive attitude. I love how kind you are to others. I even love the way you messily eat your food." Each sentence is punctuated with a kiss.

"I love you, Maris. Please come back to me."

The grip on my waist loosens, and Maris begins to shrink. I fall towards the ocean with a rush, but I'm still safely wrapped in her tentacle. My stomach drops like I'm on a roller coaster, so I close my eyes. I'm not a thrill seeker.

The cool water of the ocean envelops me up to my chest. More tentacles circle around me. When I open my eyes, Maris's golden ones gaze at me. A soft smile rests on her lips. She grabs my face and crashes her mouth to mine.

The gentle waves crash around us, but Maris holds me securely. She pulls me closer, and I encircle her waist with my thighs. Her heart thrums against my chest. I open my mouth to hers, allowing her tongue to search mine. Kissing her in the ocean is different than kissing her on dry land. She practically melts into me. Her tentacles feel more alive as they stroke and hold me.

Maris breaks our kiss with a sharp inhale. "You love me?"

"Yes, Maris. I love you."

She tucks a lock of hair behind my ear. "I love you."

Chapter 19
Maris

Alex loves me. I hold her beautiful face and pepper each adorable freckle with a kiss. Her giggles are sweeter than the finest music. I could listen to her symphony for the rest of my life if she would allow it.

But hold on.

My happiness dims slightly. Alex may love me, but does she accept the mating bond? Will I have her by my side, or will she choose to reject me? The mating bond doesn't equal love, and love doesn't equal the mating bond.

I crane my neck to look at the moon, full and heavy in the night sky.

"What are you looking at?" Alex asks, casting her eyes upward.

"The moon."

"It's pretty."

I tear my gaze away so I can witness her watching the moon. An easy smile of pure bliss lights up her face. My mate looks ethereal in the moonlight. She must make her decision tonight. My previous tactic of waiting for her to accept without pushing seems ridiculous at this moment.

She admitted she loves me; she's so close to being mine forever.

"Alex," I say gently to snag her attention.

When she looks at me, my heart swells. I never thought I would see this grumpy girl look at me with such tenderness.

It's now or never.

"Will you be my mate?"

I expect Alex to tense up at the mention of the bond like she always does. Instead, she throws back her head and laughs. I rarely see this side of Alex, and she's truly beautiful when uninhibited.

"Of course, I accept. I love you, Maris. I want to be by your side for as long as I can."

Too overjoyed to form words, I respond with a kiss. Alex kisses me back through more giggles.

"What's so funny?" I murmur against her mouth.

"I'm just happy." She snuggles her face into the crook of my neck. "I never thought I could feel this way."

The moment is interrupted by distant splashing. The monster hunters are swimming furiously towards us. I had let them go when I transformed back into my true form, hoping they would find a lifeboat and begin their journey back to where they came from, but turns out they are bigger fools than I originally thought.

"Alex," I say, my voice lowering. "There's one thing you must do to accept the bond, but we must be quick about it."

She nods, her eyes flicking between me and the approaching monster hunters. "Anything."

"You have to swallow my heart."

Alex stares at me, mouth agape. "I'm sorry. I don't think I caught that."

"You have to swallow my heart. Well, the magic of my heart. Quick before the hunters get here."

"Umm...how do you propose I do that?" She looks at me incredulously, brows creased.

I hold my hands over my heart. Closing my eyes, I concentrate. I listen to the beat of my heart and how it syncs with the tide. Everything slows down, and all other sounds fade away. I tug at the sensation.

Warmth blossoms in my palms as I pull. A fizzing sound causes me to open my eyes. Soft white light glows in my hands, reminding me of the moon. It crackles with an occasional harmless spark.

Alex gasps. "What is that?"

The light flares at the sound of her voice. "It's my heart, Alex. And it belongs to you."

"Your heart looks like the moon." She looks at my hands with wide eyes, wonderment on her face.

"It's because we are bound to the tide, which answers only to the moon."

She reaches out to touch it but draws back before her fingers can feel the heat. "And I have to swallow it?"

"Yes. Once you do, we are tied together."

The splashing of Sergeant and Georgie becomes louder. "Don't you dare eat that heart!" Sergeant screeches. "Georgie! Get that human bitch before she swallows it, or we're done for!"

I bite back a giggle. Do they really think they have an advantage here? Even if Alex weren't a lifeguard and a powerful swimmer in her own right, I'm a kraken. They would never have any success catching her.

Alex looks at me, teeth sunk into her bottom lip. "What does that mean?"

"When a human consumes a kraken's heart, they gain a

longer life," I explain. "If you accept the mating bond, it will make my heart useless to them."

"I can be with you longer?" she breathes.

"Yes."

"And we can get these monster hunters off our backs for good?"

I hadn't thought of that. All that mattered was giving my heart to Alex to seal the mating bond.

"My mate would be clever," I smirk. She's intelligent for catching on so quickly to the dire situation at hand.

Alex blushes, the faint pink visible in the light from my heart's magic. "I feel pretty stupid that I denied you for so long."

My heart flickers in my hands, hating her self-doubt. "Your reasoning made sense. Choice matters."

Her face softens. "Thank you, Maris."

I extend my arms so my heart is closer. "Take it. Make me yours."

Alex accepts the light with gentle fingers. I'm content and at home in her hands.

"And I will be yours."

The shouts of protest from the hunters as they swim closer ring out into the night, but it doesn't matter.

Alex tips her head back, brings the light to her lips, and swallows my heart.

Chapter 20
Alex

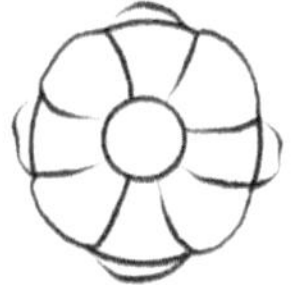

My mate's heart is warm like a cup of coffee heated to just the right temperature. As the magic slides over my tongue, I'm hit with the overwhelming sensation of dozing in sunlight on a breezy day. It's comforting, reminding me of the rare feeling of waking up after a truly restful sleep in the arms of someone who loves me. In this case, that someone is Maris.

The light settles into my chest, and the warmth spreads with each beat of my heart. It tingles through my veins, waking my body in a way I never thought possible. Every lap of water against my skin, every squeeze of Maris's tentacles, and every kiss she peppers on my face is a flood of euphoria on my senses. Once the tingling reaches every inch of my body, it dissipates, leaving a low hum in its wake.

"I love you," Maris murmurs against my mouth.

"I love you, my mate." I kiss her, drowning in the thrilling pressure of her lips on mine.

She smiles. The scrape of her fangs against my bottom lip is sensational, sending a shiver of pleasure up my spine. I thought fucking Maris was already the best physical experience I could have, but I can't wait to see what the mating bond does to our lovemaking.

I tangle my hands in her hair and grind against her, already turned on. Maris growls and grips me tighter.

"No!" Sergeant cries, pounding the water with his fist. "The kraken is fucking useless to us now. And we're stranded in the middle of the fucking ocean."

Did the damn monster hunters really have to cunt block me right now?

Georgie struggles to tread water, panting heavily. "I told you we shouldn't mess with a kraken's mate."

"Shut the fuck up! We should be thinking about how we're going to explain this shit to our buyer."

"What about how to get out of this damn ocean?"

I lean into Maris. "We should help them."

She jerks back to get a better look at my face, but I'm serious. "We can't leave them here to die," I explain.

"But they hurt you."

"Yeah. And I'm fine now."

Maris chuckles. "When did you become the positive one?"

"I guess you rubbed off on me." I roll my eyes.

"There's my grumpy girl." She tickles my sides.

A shriek of a giggle escapes my mouth. "Stop! Can we please help them?"

She sighs. "Fine. But don't expect me to be nice about it."

"There are two lifeboats over there." I point to my left. "One for us and one for them?"

"Alright. But we take care of you first."

Maris hauls me to a nearby, somehow intact lifeboat. With a quick kiss, she places me on the boat before grabbing the additional lifeboat and giving it hard shove towards the monster hunters. "You better swim for it, assholes!"

Georgie and Sergeant scramble towards the lifeline. I hold back a giggle as they struggle to climb into the boat, tipping back into the ocean several times. Right before it gets to the point where I feel kind of bad for them and almost ask Maris for help, Georgie finally hauls himself up at the right angle, before holding out a hand to Sergeant and helping him onto the boat.

"Thank you," Georgie calls to Maris between heavy pants.

Sergeant scowls, crossing his arms over his chest, and glaring at Maris.

She glares right back at him. "Am I going to regret my decision to help you?"

"Hey," I call to Maris in a low voice. "I think that's the best we're going to get from them. Especially the weird skinny one."

"But they should be groveling!" she argues, her mouth agape.

I laugh. "No need. I just want to go home, and hopefully never see or hear from them again."

Maris sneers at the hunters. "So long, assholes!" she shouts at them before turning back to me. "I think the best way to get home is for me to tug you."

"Won't you get tired?" I ask.

"Not at all." Maris flexes her biceps. "I'm a kraken! I am much stronger and faster than any human."

She's so cute. I love it when Maris is in a flirty mood, but I don't allow myself to relax just yet. There's still one little problem. "How do you know where to go?"

"I know we are somewhere in the Gulf of Mexico, but I am unsure where exactly. I'm going to follow the tide to the nearest landfall. Hopefully, it's inhabited, and we can find our way back to Sunshine Key."

"Alright." I finally allow myself a grin. "Let's go home."

Maris grips the lifeboat with two tentacles, suctioning herself to it. After a wink and a blown kiss, she dives under the water and pulls me across the water faster than I could have ever hoped to row. Having a motor and GPS would have been nice, but I trust Maris to get us safely to land.

I use the opportunity to lay back and admire the night sky. The stars are brighter in the middle of the ocean with no light pollution. The way I can actually see them twinkle is nothing short of extraordinary. I've spent so much of my life with my head down, focusing on what's directly in front of me, that I never thought to look up and dream.

The celestial body of light that monopolizes most of my attention is the moon. Maris said she's connected to the moon, and now that I share the magic of her heart, that connection glows within me. It's like she's whispering into my ear, calling me to her. I finally understand why so many civilizations and spiritualities have looked to the moon. She's wonderful and powerful.

Just as the sun begins to lighten the night sky, I see the twinkling of lights in the distance. We're close to land.

"Maris!" I shout, hoping she can hear me from under the water.

The lifeboat slows, and she pops her head above the surface. "Yes, my mate."

I point to the cluster of lights in the distance. "I think that's a city ahead of us."

"Excellent! Good keeping an eye out."

"Maybe we should row the rest of the way in. We'll likely run into fishermen soon. I bet they can radio for help." I wince. "However, there's just one little problem."

"What's that?"

"Unless we can somehow magically avoid the police, we're going to have a problem explaining your existence. You don't exactly have identification."

Maris shrugs. "Easy. We get some identification for me."

"That's not how that works," I explain with a giggle. "Hang back while I deal with the authorities, okay?"

"Alright." Maris pouts. "I miss you."

I laugh. "But I've been right here the whole time."

"But I haven't been able to hold or kiss you at all."

"Come here," I beckon her to come closer as I lean over the side of the boat.

Our lips meet in a gentle kiss.

She hums against my mouth. "Let's get this over with so we can go home."

Chapter 21
Maris

"I'm so happy to be home!" Alex exclaims as we walk up her steps, hand in hand.

I squeeze her hand. "Me too."

It's been a whirlwind since we stepped onto dry land. Not long into our rowing back to shore, fishermen found Alex, gave her a spare set of clean clothes and radioed for help. Thankfully, they didn't notice me lurking beneath the waves. It was easy to follow them back to shore.

Our little boat was discovered right outside a city called Key Biscayne. I hid under a dock and listened as the authorities questioned Alex. Ella and Avery had reported the hunters had kidnapped Alex. I let out a sigh of relief not hearing my name mentioned. They must have thought better of reporting a kraken as missing.

Alex was questioned extensively on the identity of our kidnappers. It turns out George Miller and Nicholas 'Sergeant' Wilson are wanted for leading an organized human trafficking ring. I have a feeling most of those 'humans' were monsters. Alex did her best to be as helpful as possible, which will hopefully lead to their arrests.

Eventually, the police released Alex, asking her to contact the local law enforcement in Sunshine Key for further questioning.

After Alex taking a quick stop to get some fresh clothes for me, she came back to the dock to find me and we hitched a ride back to Sunshine Key.

By the time we pulled onto Alex's street, my skin was on fire, and I can't wait to be in the water again. We drag ourselves up the stairs, exhausted and spent. When we open the door, we're greeted by Avery and Ella.

"Thank fuck!" Avery exclaims before throwing herself around me and Alex. "We've been waiting forever for you to get home."

Tears stream down Ella's face, but she hangs back, waiting her turn to greet us. But Avery pulls her in, and we hold one another in a massive group hug, relieved that our nightmare is over.

Alex is the one who finally breaks the embrace. "How are you two? Are you hurt? How did you escape?"

Despite my mate pulling away, I cling to Avery and Ella. "I'm so sorry. This is all my fault."

Ella chuckles. "I don't know who to address first."

"First of all"—Avery holds up a finger, wagging it in my face—"there's no need to apologize. The blame is on those assholes, not you. As for Alex's questions—we are fine; we aren't hurt; and once the creepy one left, we felt safe enough to wiggle out of our bonds. The big guy didn't tie us that tight, thankfully."

Alex's shoulders sag in relief. "I was so worried. I'm glad you're okay."

"Of course." Ella offers us a soft smile. "We also kept your phone charged. Avery filled in your parents, but you better call them."

"Thank you. I'll call them right away."

An itch burns my face. I fight the urge to scratch myself because I don't want to be rude and scare off my friends.

But Avery calls me out. "Why are you making that weird face, Maris? Are you feeling okay?"

I hug myself, the itch unbearable, but I don't want to scratch my skin. "I've been in this human skin and out of the water for too long."

Her eyes narrow in determination. "What can we do?"

Alex puts an arm around my shoulder. "She needs water. I have to fill up the giant garden tub in the big ensuite."

"Right." Avery nods. She turns to Ella. "Let's go so Maris can soak in peace."

"Agreed." Ella quirks an eyebrow. "Brunch tomorrow? I have to know what happened and why your eyes are extra sparkly, Alex."

Alex grins. "Yes, please! I need to stop by the police station tomorrow for questioning, but it would be great to catch up."

Avery claps her hands together. "Text me the details, so Ella and I can start cooking during your interview, okay?"

"Sounds good."

I wrap Avery and Ella in one more hug. "Thank you for being such amazing friends."

"Of course, Maris." Avery squeezes me hard. "You're family now." When she pulls away, she shoots me a knowing wink.

She must have realized Alex accepted the mating bond since I'm not dying. I debate if I should tell Alex that I almost died because of her hesitation, but I decide against it. That knowledge would only make her feel guilty. Maybe someday. But not when it's so fresh.

As soon as Avery and Ella close the door behind them with enthusiastic farewells, Alex grabs my wrist and leads me down the hall to the bedroom. She turns the faucet so the tub can start filling.

"I'm going to step out and call my parents. I'll be back in a few," she explains, walking out of the bathroom.

I bite my lip to keep from pouting. Being apart from Alex is excruciating, especially considering we just sealed the bond. All I want is to be as close to her as possible. But I'm going to have to restrain myself. There is more to her world than just me, so I use the opportunity to take a few deep breaths and thank the Goddess for bringing Alex into my life.

The moment she swallowed my heart, I felt complete. I now belong to Alex entirely and totally. She's as tied to me as I am to her. When a human consumes a kraken heart, they gain a longer life, but that's when it's taken without consent by someone who isn't a mate, and the kraken is dead. But I know now that Alex consuming my heart has made her mortal life immortal. I don't know how she'll respond to such a revelation. Living forever is daunting.

"Alright! I am off the hook for the rest of the night," Alex sings, skipping back into the bathroom.

"I have you all to myself?"

She giggles and kneels next to the bath. "Yes. All yours."

I take her hands in mine. "I need to tell you something."

Alex's smile drops. "What is it?"

"You know how when a human swallows a kraken heart, they live longer?"

"Yes?" She chews her lip.

"Because I gave my heart willingly to my mate, you're now as immortal as I am."

Her eyes widen. "How do you know that?"

I place a hand over her chest. "Can't you feel it?"

She places her hands under mine and closes her eyes. A low hum emits from between her pursed lips. When Alex finally opens her eyes, they gleam with knowledge. "I feel it."

"Come here." I pull her face closer to mine, examining her eyes. This is the first opportunity I've had to focus on them.

Ella is right. Alex's eyes sparkle with something otherworldly. It's subtle and not something you would notice unless you looked closely. Upon closer inspection, I see the moon. The celestial being that ties me to this earth is in her eyes. She is truly a kraken's mate now.

"Do you accept that the earth may die before you do?" I ask.

Alex leans in, pressing her lips against mine. "As long as you're by my side."

I rise in the tub to gain better access to her mouth, sloshing water onto the floor. "Whoops! Sorry."

Her laugh is carefree. "Don't worry about it." Alex rises from her knees and begins unbuttoning her shirt. "Do you care if I join you?"

Chapter 22
Alex

Maris's tender gaze becomes hazy with lust. "I would love nothing more than for you to join me."

I attempt my best sultry pout as I strip off my shirt. If I look awkward, Maris doesn't let on. She gazes at me like a woman dying of thirst, discovering a cold, fresh-water spring. It's exhilarating to have this mythical creature in the palm of my hand.

Maris sucks in a sharp inhale when I unzip my salt-encrusted shorts to reveal the top of my boxer briefs. A smirk forms on my lip as I continue to tease her by slowly dragging my shorts down my hips. I peel off my underwear while holding her gaze. Maris's tentacles writhe in desire, indicating just how bad she wants me.

Once I'm completely nude, Maris takes her time drinking in my body. "You are a goddess."

Heat flushes my entire body pink. "You are closer to a goddess than me."

Maris's eyes narrow. "I won't allow you to speak ill of my mate."

I giggle. "You're ridiculous."

"But you still love me." Her expression is smug, too smug for my liking. She's always in control of our intimate moments. Now it's my turn.

I muster up all my confidence, which isn't difficult when Maris can't take her lascivious gaze off me. "If you want to call me a goddess, I'll have you treating me like one before the night is over."

She smirks. "Is that a provocation?"

"Do you dare challenge your goddess?" I saunter towards her. It's my turn to look smug when her throat bobs.

"What are you going to do to me?"

"Whatever I please," I purr as I climb into the tub.

Water overflows onto the floor, but I don't care. I settle between her tentacles, which try to wrap around me, but I push them away.

"Not until I tell you to, do you understand?" I chastise.

Something primal flashes across Maris's face. But despite a low growl and heated stare, she obeys and doesn't touch me.

I gently grasp one of her tentacles and run my fingers over the suckers. Maris lets out a breathy moan. Encouraged, I bring my mouth to a sucker and pepper it with kisses. A shudder runs through her body. I circle the sucker with my tongue, treating it like I would a human clit.

"Alex!" Maris groans, her tentacles wrapping around my wrist.

"What did I tell you?" I scold, pulling away from her tentacle.

She lets me go. "Sorry!" she murmurs.

"Good girl," I coo.

Maris screws her eyes shut and takes a few deep breaths. "This is too much."

I lick up her tentacle. "Do you like what I'm doing?"

Her eyes open. "Fuck, Alex! Of course! I'm trying not to come."

"Sit back and relax. I'm taking care of you tonight." I wrap my mouth around her tentacle and suck.

Maris's hips buck, but I grip them, forcing them to be still. I'm calling the shots tonight.

She moans as I suck and lick her tentacle. This isn't the first time I've pleasured her like this, but it is the first time I'm in control of how deep it goes. I take her to the back of my throat, nearly gagging at the intrusion. Using my hands, I work up and down her tentacle. Her breathing becomes more labored, and her other five tentacles and hands grip the edge of the tub. I've never felt sexier.

Maris writhes, unable to remain still. "Alex! I'm going to come!"

I encourage her to orgasm by taking her deeper. She grabs a fistful of my hair with one hand and uses the other to push back any covering my face. I let her, wanting to see my mouth around her tentacle. With one last suck, Maris yelps a moan, reaching her peak. Her tentacle swells, and I relax my jaw to accommodate her.

I rub my thighs together, remembering the way she filled me the other night. I want that again. With a wet pop, I remove her tentacle from my mouth. "How was that?"

"Incredible," Maris pants. Her hands are still tangled in my hair, but her grip has relaxed.

"Are you ready for another one?"

A mischievous glint flashes in her eyes. "Only if you come too."

I smirk, taking a tentacle in my hand and rubbing it against my entrance. "Are you talking back to your goddess?"

Maris smirks, shaking her head. "Whatever you say."

"That's what I thought." I adjust my hips, sinking her tentacle into me.

We moan in unison. A gentle thrumming causes my entire body to quiver.

"What the fuck?" I groan. "I thought you felt good before, but now I feel like I'm vibrating."

"It's the mating bond," Maris murmurs in my ear.

And I nearly come undone at the gentle tickle from her breath.

"It's glorious, isn't it?"

"I've never felt anything like this." I start to rock my hips, fascinated by how much more I can feel every texture of her tentacle.

"You look so beautiful riding my tentacle. You are indeed a goddess."

"Maris!" I huff.

"Yes, my goddess?"

"Make love to me."

A second tentacle latches onto my clit while two more squeeze my breasts as they suck my nipples. Another one suctions to my asshole. *Fuck.* Nothing compares to having every erogenous zone stimulated at the same time. I continue to ride Maris as her final tentacle enters my mouth.

Yes. This is what I want. I want to feel as much of Maris as I can. The thrumming increases in frequency, igniting something hot but not unpleasant under my skin. Every nerve ending is alive. Every time I bounce on her tentacles, she matches my pace and pressure. We are in sync, chasing each other to climax.

"My mate, my beautiful goddess," Maris moans. "I want to feel you come around me."

My orgasm is fast approaching, coming at me like a tsunami. With a massive crash, I'm clenching my pussy around Maris's tentacle.

She's not far behind me. "Alex! You feel magnificent," Maris cries as she swells inside me.

A damp haze blurs my vision. She's once again making me come so hard that I'm crying. I let out a muffled sob around the tentacle in my mouth. The heat in my chest roars like a fire doused with gasoline before sputtering to a dull ember as I come down from my climax.

Maris eases her tentacles from me and then promptly collapses. "Oh fuck, Alex. That was sensational."

I wipe the tears from my cheek. "If I had known orgasms would feel like that I would have accepted the mating bond the first night," I admit with a chuckle.

"You're a cruel goddess," Maris teases.

A tingle shivers up my spine as a tentacle twitches between my thighs. "Why am I already aroused again?"

Her grin is sheepish as her cheeks darken. "It's the mating frenzy."

"The what now?"

"Mating frenzy. It'll pass. It's easiest to give in to it, but I'm happy to restrain myself if you wish."

"Oh, I'm giving in." I sit up in the tub. "But first, I'm starving. Can we take a snack break?"

Maris giggles. "I thought you would never ask."

We climb out of the tub, careful to avoid slipping in the massive puddle we created in our loving making.

"I'm sorry about your floors," Maris says, eyes wide at the mess.

"Totally worth it." I wring out my wet hair. "What do you want for a snack?"

"I could go for some salmon and eggs." She rubs a hand over her stomach.

"Cooked?"

She shoots me a devilish grin. "Normally, I would love to eat your delicious cooked eggs, but I'll take them raw tonight to save time. I'm more hungry for your body than food."

I laugh. "I understand."

Together, we walk hand in hand to the kitchen. Maris takes the last of the eggs and salmon steaks. I'll have to find time to go to the grocery store in the middle of this mating frenzy. Or maybe I'll get the groceries delivered.

I quickly assemble a peanut butter sandwich and grab a banana before following Maris to the bedroom. Usually, I have a strict 'no food where I sleep' rule, but I can't stand to waste another minute not being in bed with my mate.

"Are you seriously bringing a banana with you?" Maris wrinkles her nose.

"Of course. Bananas are delicious." I take a large bite of the fruit just to prove my point.

She sticks her tongue out. "No. They're disgusting."

I grin, my mouth still full. "You're lucky I love you."

My mate surprises me by leaning and pressing her lips against mine. There's no way she didn't taste the banana. But she doesn't make a disgusted face.

Instead, she smiles. "I know."

Epilogue
Alex

"Where's Maris?" Avery asks, bursting through the front door of my home unannounced.

I can't be too mad. It is Christmas, and I'm the one who gave her a key to mine and Maris's new house.

"She said she had to meet Ella somewhere." I shrug.

Avery scowls. "She better get her tentacled ass back here before Mom and Dad arrive with the pies. A girl is ready to eat."

"Hopefully this Christmas will be better than last year's," I mutter.

Avery nudges me with her elbow. "Last year, you sprung that your new girlfriend is a kraken on our parents. So, unless you have any other secrets, we should be fine."

Mom and Dad freaked out when I told them about Maris's true identity last Christmas. I don't blame them. They found out their daughter's partner was a legendary sea monster. But this Christmas will be different. They already know and have accepted Maris for who she is, and they even ended up taking the fact that I'm now immortal pretty well.

I'm excited for this year. Maris and I bought a new house with a private entrance to a canal and a saltwater pool, so she has easy access to the best water for her daily soaks. I will forever be grateful that when she recovered her memories, she also remembered the location of her den, which was chock-full of treasure.

When Maris brought up chest after chest of gold and jewels, I was speechless for hours. What were we going to do with all that money?

"There's more where that came from," she said. "But I think we should keep some hidden in my den, just in case."

I agreed, dumbfounded by the amount of wealth Maris had buried away.

It was a headache getting the treasure appraised. There were a lot of questions about how we'd come into possession of such antiques, but when you live on an island, scuba diving is always an easy excuse. Once we found a reliable dealer from the mainland, Maris and I were set for a lifetime.

We could buy a new home with the money and pay to keep my parents' house ready for them whenever they came home from RVing around the country. I also decided to finally follow my passion and start up an interior design business, helping aesthetically challenged homeowners around The Keys. Word has even spread to the mainland, and I have a client in Miami who wants to meet with me after the holidays.

As for my job as a pool manager? I gave up my position, allowing Carter to take the reins. I must admit I was worried about him being the manager, but I've heard from old coworkers that he matured into the role. I'm proud of him. Still mad at what he did to Ella, but proud.

After going through a few seedy channels, we acquired

a set of fake documents for Maris, just in case. She now spends her time taking care of our household and trying various 'exciting human hobbies,' from model building and scrapbooking to gardening and knitting. We can't risk her getting a job in case the stress or the time away from the water forces her to transform. Any jobs at a pool or around the ocean are a no-go. She still can't control transforming as soon as she's submerged in water. I don't mind. We have plenty of money, and I like having all the free time I want with my mate.

To say life is good is an understatement. Being in love has completed me in a way I never thought possible. It also doesn't hurt that I share the heart of my mate. We grow closer every day, sometimes able to communicate without uttering a single word to each other. Avery calls it 'creepy,' but Maris and I don't care.

I'm startled from my romantic thoughts by Mom and Dad's polite knock before entering. They fawn over the massive 12-foot tree adorned in tasteful blue and silver ornaments and ribbons. Eat your heart out, Better Homes and Gardens. Avery bustles around the kitchen, basting the ham and arranging the sides and pies on the table.

"Where is that kraken?" she bellows. "I'm starving!"

I scoff. "She'll be here any minute."

My mom pats my hand. "Maybe you should call her, dear. You know how your sister gets when she's hungry."

I frown, but Mom is right. If Avery doesn't eat soon, she's going to lose her shit. I snatch my phone from the couch, and I'm about to dial Maris when the front door flies open.

My mate holds a wooden milk crate in her arms. When she sees my parents, her face breaks out in a huge grin. "I'm so happy to see you! Sorry for being late." She sheds her human glamor, appearing in all her beautiful kraken glory.

"You better be sorry!" Avery calls from the kitchen. "If this ham is dry because of your tardiness, I won't let you have any of the crab legs I boiled just for you."

I roll my eyes. "You know how Avery gets when she's hungry."

Maris giggles, and the milk crate shifts in her arms.

"Is that what you had to get from Ella?" I quirk an eyebrow, curious as to why it would move on its own.

"Yes!" Maris sets the crate on the floor. "She was keeping your Christmas present for me."

"My present?"

"Open it!" Maris squeals.

My family gathers around. What kind of gift would a kraken give for Christmas?

A soft mewl reaches my ears when I remove the lid. Inside, is a large, orange tabby cat with glittering green eyes. Everyone coos over him, calling him a 'handsome man' and a 'good kitty.'

"Is this Tommy?" I squeak, recognizing him from the shelter.

Maris nods. "I know we've been wanting to adopt a senior cat for a while, but you kept hesitating. You really hit it off with Tommy, so I adopted him. He's been living with Ella for the past few days."

Tears spring to my eyes. "This is my gift?" I lift Tommy out of the crate. His fur is as soft as I remember.

"If you decide he's not the cat for you, Ella has agreed to keep him."

I gasp in mock horror, clutching Tommy to my chest. "Never. This is my little baby man."

A proud smile spreads across Maris's face. "You mean 'our' little baby man."

"Sure," I agree, waving her off. My mind is already scheming ways to make Tommy comfortable and happy. I give him a few scratches under the chin.

"I already bought his necessities. I hid them in the guest room closet, but I figured tomorrow we could pick out his accessories."

"Really?" My face lights up, imagining Tommy in a blue collar with a gold bell.

Maris nods, popping a kiss on top of our cat's head. "Welcome to your new home, Tommy."

I rest my head on my mate's shoulder. "Thank you, Maris. He's wonderful. I love him already."

Avery huffs. "Okay, this moment is cute and all, but when can we eat?"

Maris chuckles. "I'll show him his litter box real quick. You join your family at the table before your sister has an aneurysm."

"I heard that!" Avery snaps.

I roll my eyes. "Hurry! And bring Tommy with you. I miss him already."

Maris presses her lips to mine, but when she pulls away, I grab her by the back of the neck and bring her to me for a deeper kiss.

"I love you," I murmur against her mouth.

She looks at me, eyes shimmering with tenderness; no words are needed to convey her feelings for me. But she says them anyway. "Not as much as I love you."

I hum in response. Nothing on this earth is like a kraken's devotion to her mate.

Acknowledgments

I can't believe I actually get to write an acknowledgments page for a book. This is a childhood dream come true. I would have never gotten here without the help and support from my amazing community of friends and supporters. Where to even start? There are just so many people who helped make this labor of love possible.

I have to start with Iris. You've been here for me for years, helping me improve my writing. I've learned so much from you, and somehow, you always remain patient with me, gently leading me in the right direction.

The only reason I didn't fall apart during this whole process was because I had Lexie in my corner. I never would have made it through this without you. Your insight, knowledge, and support were a flashlight in the dark.

Whenever I felt down in the dumps about myself, I thought about Lizzy, the first person to read Sink Into Her in its entirety. Your comments and enthusiasm for my story and characters kept me going. I especially appreciate your excitement over the smutty scenes.

This book wouldn't have a title without Sasha. Seriously, babe, thank you so much for using that beautiful brain of yours to name Sink Into Her. You know you have to help me with future book titles now, right?

My characters would have swum in my head forever if it wasn't for Zoë. I will never forget your incredible creative insight as you brought my characters to life. Maris and Alex exist because of you! I look forward to bringing future characters to life with you.

Honestly, where would I even be without my beta readers? Morgi, not only were your comments hilarious and made me smile for days, but you also gave me amazing insight into how others would perceive my story. Zeke, you know how much I respect you as a writer, so any crumb of praise you gave me left me elated. Heather, I was so happy the day you reached out to me. Your feedback was incredibly valuable to me.

Who else remembers the names for all the tenses? Not me. At least I didn't, until Sarah came along. Thank you for being such a helpful editor who educated me. I'm confident I'm a better writer now because of you.

My sweet, sweet, amazingly skilled Kiiryn. Before I even started writing this book, I knew I wanted you to make the art for my cover. You did not disappoint.

The first person to know I was even contemplating writing a book was my oldest friend, Deanna. Did you ever think that we would be here 20 years ago? You always know exactly what to say to encourage me past my self-doubt. I seriously couldn't have done this without your support.

And last but definitely not least, I can't wrap this up without thanking my wife. All the late-night plot hole talks, picking up my slack while I worked on this story, feedback on random pages, and the never-ending supply of hugs made this possible. Thank you. I love you.

About the Author

Elaine J. Daniels writes the stories she wants to read. For as long as she can remember, she has imagined vivid characters with extraordinary lives and adventures. Her first attempt at writing a novel was a retelling of Lord of the Rings with herself as the protagonist (and Frodo's girlfriend) when she was 11. When she's not writing, Elaine enjoys reading romance novels, eating her wife's cooking, trying new hobbies, and spending quality time with her friends, family, and furry babies.